"IT'S TRULY EXTRAORDINARY," HE SAID . . .

"Who would believe it? 'Jewish girl risks all for German soldier.' Tell me, Patty Bergen"—his voice became soft, but with a trace of hoarseness—"why are you doing this for me?"

It wasn't complicated. Why didn't he know? There was really only one word for it. A simple little word that in itself is reason enough . . .

SUMMER OF MY GERMAN SOLDIER

Bette Greene's award-winning novel
The story of a very special friendship

"Courageous and compelling!"

—**Publishers Weekly**

Bantam Books by Louis L'Amour
Ask your bookseller for the books you have missed

NOVELS

BENDIGO SHAFTER
BORDEN CHANTRY
BRIONNE
THE BROKEN GUN
THE BURNING HILLS
THE CALIFORNIOS
CALLAGHEN
CATLOW
CHANCY
THE CHEROKEE TRAIL
COMSTOCK LODE
CONAGHER
CROSSFIRE TRAIL
DARK CANYON
DOWN THE LONG HILLS
THE EMPTY LAND
FAIR BLOWS THE WIND
FALLON
THE FERGUSON RIFLE
THE FIRST FAST DRAW
FLINT
GUNS OF THE TIMBERLANDS
HANGING WOMAN CREEK
THE HAUNTED MESA
HELLER WITH A GUN
THE HIGH GRADERS
HIGH LONESOME
HONDO
HOW THE WEST WAS WON
THE IRON MARSHAL
THE KEY-LOCK MAN
KID RODELO
KILKENNY
KILLOE
KILRONE
KIOWA TRAIL
LAST OF THE BREED
LAST STAND AT PAPAGO WELLS
THE LONESOME GODS
THE MAN CALLED NOON
THE MAN FROM SKIBBEREEN
THE MAN FROM THE BROKEN HILLS
MATAGORDA
MILO TALON
THE MOUNTAIN VALLEY WAR
NORTH TO THE RAILS
OVER ON THE DRY SIDE
PASSIN' THROUGH
THE PROVING TRAIL
THE QUICK AND THE DEAD
RADIGAN
REILLY'S LUCK
THE RIDER OF LOST CREEK
RIVERS WEST
THE SHADOW RIDERS
SHALAKO
SHOWDOWN AT YELLOW BUTTE

SILVER CANYON
SITKA
SON OF A WANTED MAN
TAGGART
THE TALL STRANGER
TO TAME A LAND
TUCKER
UNDER THE SWEETWATER RIM
UTAH BLAINE
THE WALKING DRUM
WESTWARD THE TIDE
WHERE THE LONG GRASS BLOWS

SHORT STORY COLLECTIONS

BOWDRIE
BOWDRIE'S LAW
BUCKSKIN RUN
DUTCHMAN'S FLAT
THE HILLS OF HOMICIDE
LAW OF THE DESERT BORN
LONG RIDE HOME
LONIGAN
NIGHT OVER THE SOLOMONS
THE RIDER OF THE RUBY HILLS
RIDING FOR THE BRAND
THE STRONG SHALL LIVE
THE TRAIL TO CRAZY MAN
WAR PARTY
WEST FROM SINGAPORE
YONDERING

SACKETT TITLES

SACKETT'S LAND
TO THE FAR BLUE MOUNTAINS
THE WARRIOR'S PATH
JUBAL SACKETT
RIDE THE RIVER
THE DAYBREAKERS
SACKETT
LANDO
MOJAVE CROSSING
MUSTANG MAN
THE LONELY MEN
GALLOWAY
TREASURE MOUNTAIN
LONELY ON THE MOUNTAIN
RIDE THE DARK TRAIL
THE SACKETT BRAND
THE SKY-LINERS

NONFICTION

FRONTIER
EDUCATION OF A WANDERING MAN
THE SACKETT COMPANION: A Personal
   Guide to the Sackett Novels
A TRAIL OF MEMORIES: The Quotations
   of Louis L'Amour, compiled by
   Angelique L'Amour

Summer
of My
German Soldier

Bette Greene

GRE (pbk)

BC # 674

BANTAM BOOKS
NEW YORK · TORONTO · LONDON · SYDNEY · AUCKLAND

This edition contains the complete text
of the original hardcover edition.
NOT ONE WORD HAS BEEN OMITTED.

RL 5, IL age 11 and up

SUMMER OF MY GERMAN SOLDIER
*A Bantam Book / published by arrangement with
The Dial Press*

PRINTING HISTORY
*Dial edition published October 1973
2nd printing . . . March 1974
Bantam edition / November 1974
23 printings through October 1988*

1

WHEN I SAW the crowd gathering at the train station, I worried what President Roosevelt would think. I just hope he doesn't get the idea that Jenkinsville, Arkansas, can't be trusted with a military secret because, truth of the matter is, we're as patriotic as anybody.

In front of the station house five or six Boy Scouts in full uniform circled their leader, Jimmy Wells, who was wearing the same expression Dane Clark wore as the Marine sergeant in *Infamy at Pearl Harbor*. "This is the situation, guys," Jimmy said. "The sheriff told me it's the Army's job to get the Nazis off the train and into the prison camp, but I figger they'll be mighty glad to have us Scouts on hand. And if any of those rats try to make a getaway"—he slapped the leather-encased Scout ax strapped to his waist—"we know what to do."

I looked around for a friendly group to join. Mary Wren was holding onto the arm of Reverend Benn's wife as though that was going to provide her with the Lord's own protection. There are plenty of jokes going around about our town's telephone operator. People say Mary is so generous that she'll give you the gossip right off her tongue.

Then I saw old Chester, the colored porter from my father's store, closing his eyes against the brilliant June sun.

I walked over. "Hey, Chester, don't you think this is the most exciting thing that has ever happened to our town?"

His eyes jerked open. "I'm going back to the stock room right now, Miss Patty. Ain't been gone more'n two, maybe three minutes."

"Don't go on account of me, Chester. I won't tell my father. Honest." Chester smiled wide enough to show his gold tooth. "I've never in my whole life seen a German, I mean, in person. Have you?"

"I seen some foreigners once, but they was fortune-telling gypsies."

I looked over to where Sheriff Cauldwell, Mr. George C. Henkins, the president of the Jenkinsville Rotary Club, and Mr. Quentin Blakey, editor of the *Rice County Gazette,* were standing on the gray-white gravel. "I wonder what the sheriff is saying about all this," I said, heading toward them.

Mr. Blakey's head was pitched back to look into the sun-and-leather face of the sheriff. "I said, 'Captain, I know you're only doing your job as a public information officer, but I'll never understand why I'm not supposed to write about what everybody here already knows about.' "

"That's telling him, Quent," said the sheriff, looking amused.

"More to it than that," said Mr. Blakey. "Captain wouldn't tell me how many POW camps there are or where they're located, but after a while he forgot about security—told me that up in Boston they got a bunch of Italian prisoners who do nothing but clean up after the elephants in Franklin Park."

Sheriff Cauldwell leaned his big head back and laughed the laugh of the healthy. "Captain wasn't talking security, he was talking crap."

From down the tracks, a whistle. Jimmy Wells ran over to one of the rails, dropped to his knees, and pressed his ear against it. His features were molded

2

into Dane Clark's odds-are-against-us-but-we-can-do-it expression as he announced, "She's a-coming!"

All talking stopped and the small clusters of people began merging into one single mass. Even Chester, the only Negro, was now standing in arm-touching contact with whites.

Then amid hissing, steamy clouds of white, the train braked, screeched, and finally came to a halt.

From the crowd a woman's voice—it may have been Reverend Benn's wife—asked, "Well, where are they?"

Jimmy Wells pointed to the last passenger car. "There!"

Everyone hurried toward the end of the train in time to see two GIs with their side arms still strapped in their holsters step quickly from the car. Then came the Germans. The crowd moved back slightly, leaving a one-person-wide path between themselves and the train.

The prisoners were unhandcuffed, unchained young men carrying regulation Army duffel bags. They wore fresh blue denim pants and matching shirts, and if it hadn't been for the black "POW" stenciled across their shirt backs you could easily have mistaken them for an ordinary crew from the Arkansas Public Works Department sent out to repair a stretch of highway. I tried to read their faces for brutality, terror, humiliation—something. But the only thing I sensed was a kind of relief at finally having arrived at their destination.

"Nazis!" A woman's voice shouted. And this time I knew for sure that it was Mrs. Benn.

A blond prisoner who was stepping off the train at that moment stopped short then smiled and waved. It was as though he believed, or wanted to believe, that Mrs. Benn's call was nothing more than a friendly American greeting.

3

I raised my hand, but before I completed a full wave Mary Wren pressed it down, shaking her head.

"I'm sorry, but I didn't think it would be polite—I guess I just forgot," I said, wondering if I was going to be served up as the main course for Mary Wren's gossip of the day.

The last two prisoners stepped off the train—there were fifteen or sixteen, maybe twenty in all. After them came two more American guards, one a sergeant. As the procession walked down the gravel slope to the waiting Army truck Jimmy Wells tapped on the sleeve of the American sergeant. "You mean this is all the Jerries we're gonna get?"

"Don't worry, son," said the sergeant. "We're gonna keep you folks well supplied. Most of them have already been transported here by truck caravan."

The prisoners and then the GIs climbed aboard the canvas-covered vehicle. At the highway it made a right turn and, shifting gears noisily, disappeared from sight.

And so I had seen it; all there was to see. Yet I felt a nagging disappointment as though something were missing. In the movies war criminals being hustled off to prison would be dramatic. Their ravaged faces would tell a story of defeat, disgrace, and downfall. But in real life it didn't seem all that important. Not really a big deal. My stomach growled, reminding me that it must be nearing lunchtime. I followed the railroad embankment toward home, walking sometimes between the tracks and sometimes only on one track, balancing like a tightrope walker.

I passed everybody's back yard: the Rhodes's, the Reeves's, the Benns', their laundry blowing on the line. The reverend wears striped boxer-style shorts, and the Mrs. has very heavy bosoms. Her bras look like a *D* cup to me.

Parallel to our Victory Garden I ran down the embankment past the lettuce, sweet corn, and tomatoes. The government says that until victory is won every-

4

body with a bit of land should grow their own food. Now, I know my father's patriotic all right, but he's not doing exactly what the government asked us to do. A colored man, Grover, is the one who did the planting.

I could see Ruth on the back porch, squeezing the clothes through the wringer. She is the color of hot chocolate before the marshmallow bleeds in. Sometimes I hear my mother telling her to lose weight. "It's not healthy to be fat." But she isn't actually fat; it's just that she has to wear large sizes. I mean, it wouldn't be Ruth if she were like my mother. And another thing, a little extra weight keeps a person warm inside.

"Hey, Ruth!" She looked up from her wash. "Ruth, know where I was? With the Germans going to the prison camp!"

She gave me her have-you-been-up-to-some-devilment look.

"I didn't do a single thing wrong!" I said, wondering if my wave would count against me. I decided that it wouldn't. "This is still my week to be good and sweet. I haven't forgotten."

Her face opened wide enough to catch the sunshine. "I'm mighty pleased to hear it. 'Cause before this week is through, your mamma and daddy gonna recognize your natural sweetness and give you some back, and then you is gonna return even more and—"

"Maybe so," I interrupted her, and she went back to putting bed sheets through the wringer, understanding that I didn't want to talk about them anymore.

"There was this sergeant guarding the prisoners—you should have seen his medals. I'm going to pray for Robert tonight, that he comes home with lots of medals—more than Jimmy Wells."

"Jimmy Wells?" Ruth repeated the name as though she hadn't heard right. "Jimmy Wells ain't no soldier!"

"No, but he must have about every medal that the Boy Scouts know how to give."

5

"Well, I don't care nothing about no wars and no medals, I jest cares about my boy coming back safe."

I wanted to tell her she had to care, how important it was for us to win this war. Put an end to Nazism forever! But I could see that Ruth's heart was too troubled to enter into that kind of discussion, so I just said again I'd remember Robert in my prayers.

A slow smile spread across her face and I found myself smiling too. See, I congratulated myself, I don't always do everything wrong.

"Go bring Sharon in from the sandpile," said Ruth. "I'll fix us up some good ole wienies and beans for lunch."

"Oh, I don't think I want any."

"Don't you go telling me what you don't be wanting, Miss Skin-and-Bones."

"Am not! As a matter of fact, if you haven't noticed, I'm really quite formidable." I exposed teeth, squinted eyes, and fashioned claws out of my hands. "Terribly and ferociously formidable!"

"That today's word?" asked Ruth.

"Yes. Isn't it grand? It means 'exciting fear or dread.' Like it?"

"I likes it right well," said Ruth thoughtfully. "But I think one of my best favorites is one of them from last month. 'Cause one night after I got home and fixed up some supper for Claude and me and cleaned up my kitchen, I got to noticing my shelf paper was getting a mite yellow so I says I better take care of it right now. Claude says leave it for another time 'cause it's pretty near to seven o'clock and I bees needing my rest. And I says Claude, you is right, but trouble is you done married a fastidious wife. A real *fastidious* wife."

My sister was sitting straight up in the sandpile, shoveling sand over her legs. Sharon's not yet six—exactly five years and ten months. But whatever she does seems to have, at least to her, a kind of purpose.

6

"Hey, Sharon," I called, "where are your legs?"

She giggled like she knew something I didn't. "Under the sand, silly."

"Are you absolutely sure? 'Cause once I had a friend named John Paul Jones, and John Paul put both legs under a lot of sand and when he went to pull them out—no legs. All those hungry little sand bugs had eaten them right off."

Sharon lifted her legs straight into the air. She seemed enormously pleased. "Well, I've still got mine. See?"

In the center of the square, breakfast-room table a bunch of back-yard roses lounged in a flowered glass that had once held pimento cheese Ruth carried in steaming plates of wienies and beans and some cut-up tomatoes lettuce, and radishes from our Victory Garden. I found my appetite.

Ruth gave Sharon a nod. "Your time to be asking the Lord's Blessing."

Immediately, without thinking, I said my own silent prayer: Please, dear God, don't let my father come in now. Amen.

Sharon clasped her hands tight. "We sure do thank you, dear Lord, for all the food we're going to eat up. Amen."

"Amen, Lord," echoed Ruth.

I heard myself sigh. I think maybe I worry too much. After all, it's just plumb silly to think of him walking in on us right in the middle of our prayers. But what could happen is that Sharon might just mention it. "Christian prayers in my house!" The nerve at his temple would pulsate. Shouts of "God damn you," directed at me and maybe at Ruth.

It's not that he's against praying or anything. Before the gasoline rationing I used to go to Jewish Sunday school at the Beth Zion Synagogue in Memphis, so I know that Jews pray too. My father asked those people down at the Ration Board for some extra stamps, but Mr. Raymond Hubbard said that he thought eighty miles round trip was a long ways to go praying and he couldn't in good conscience consider it a priority item.

"I made up some Jell-O for you," said Ruth, eyeing my empty plate.

"Uhhh, no thanks. I'm all filled up."

"I made it jest the way you like it." Her voice had softened. "It's got bananas and nuts and cut-up bits of marshmellers."

"I'll have a little. Did you, really and truly, make it especially for me?"

"Only this morning I asks myself what would Patty specially like for dessert. Then I tells myself the answer. And now you have your answer too." Ruth leaned back her head to let out a chuckle that was a full octave and a half down from middle *C*.

My sister took up the laugh. And her top-of-the-octave laugh struck me funny, and then everything was. That's the way it is with Ruth, Sharon, and me. It isn't that our jokes are all that great; it's like Ruth says, "We keep our jubilee in easy reach." Why can't it be that way with my mother and father? "Show them your natural sweetness," Ruth reminds me, " 'cause ants ain't the only thing sweetness attracts."

I looked out the window at the summer green and wished for winter white. An Alaskan blizzard with wild winds hurling ice darts onto head-high drifts. For four days and four nights the two of them have been isolated in the store. The power is down, the oil pipes have burst, and there is no food and no water.

Ruth pleads with me not to try to reach them. "You ain't gonna save them; you is only going to kill yourself dead!"

"Fill the thermos with hot soup," I tell her.

Seven times I think I can't go on. The drifts too high, my feet and face beyond any feeling. But I do go on and

8

on and on, and finally I make it. I feed them soup and tuna-fish sandwiches, and when they regain their strength they tell me how much they love me—how much they have always loved me.

"What you expecting to see out that window?" asked Ruth "The Second Coming of the Lord?"

Never would I want her to suspect me of dreaming of a miracle. "I was just thinking I might take a walk down to the store. See what's cooking."

She didn't look exactly thrilled by my idea.

"Isn't it you who's always reminding me to be sweet? Now what could be more thoughtful than bringing them up-to-the-minute war news?" They would like that too. Doesn't my father listen to the five-minute news with his neck jutting out towards the radio? And when H.V. Kaltenborn comes on I swear if his nose isn't just about touching the cloth-covered speaker.

Ruth dropped her head into the U between her thumb and her first finger. "I expect you spent the morning advising President Roosevelt on where to send his armies. That where you got your up-to-the-second war news?"

"If you don't think a hundred ferocious Nazi prisoners arriving at the Jenkinsville depot is war news then I don't know what is."

On Ruth's face was the dawning of a smile. "Got some sweetness to go with your up-to-the-second news?"

I stood up. "Maybe you oughta spend a little time telling my father and mother to serve some sweetness to me."

"Reckon they'd listen?"

"Guess not."

Ruth nodded her agreement. "Could you tell this old lady why you is always talking about your father when all the other young girls be talking about their daddies?"

9

"Well, daddies act one way and fathers act another. And anyway, I don't happen to be a young girl. I've been a teenager already for two years."

She laughed. "Oh, Honey Babe, how can you be a teenager when you is only twelve?"

" 'Cause I've been one since I was ten. Not many people know this, Ruth, but teenage actually starts when you get two numbers to your age. See?"

I could tell that it hadn't convinced her. "Don't you see, ten is in reality tenteen. Now people don't generally go around calling it tenteen cause it sounds too much like the chewing gum, but that's the only reason."

The smile that Ruth had been holding in suddenly broke through. "Honey, you jest all the time go round making up rules to suit yourself. I got myself two big numbers to my age and I shore ain't no teenager."

"Well, I can explain that. When you have two numbers to your age, you're either teenage or after teenage. And you just happen to be after teenage, understand?"

"I think I'm beginning to see the light and I do 'preciate the kind explanation, little Miss Genius."

"Make fun of me and I'll stop talking to you."

"Can't good friends kid each other a little? Make each other smile?"

"I guess so. I've got to go to the store now."

"Hold up a pretty minute, Patty. I want you to do me a mighty big favor only you can do."

I tried to hide my pleasure that somebody needed a favor only I could do.

"I want you to take off them faded old shorts and put on one of them nice pretty dresses of yours."

Sounds of my mother! "For God's sake, why do I have to get all dressed up to go to the store? I'm coming right back."

"Pride, Patty Babe, you gotta have pride."

Pride. Maybe that's it, what Ruth has. What makes her different. Keeps her from looking down at her shoes when talking with white people. Then it is all a lie what they say about her. Ruth isn't one bit uppity. Merely prideful.

"Is that why you wear a Sunday dress to walk back and forth to work?"

"That's right," she said, looking pleased that I had caught on so quickly. "It's the pride. It's me shouting out to the world that one of God's creatures is walking on by. You think God would like it if we went and used the Good Book for a doorstop?"

I shook my head No.

"Well, now, you think he bees liking it one bit better if one of his creatures be going round in dirty, worn-out clothes? You understands that, Patty?"

"I guess so."

As I crossed Main Street, the heels of my sandals made slight half-moon impressions in the hot asphalt pavement and I remembered what I'd heard said about heat at noon. "Hot by noon; Hades by afternoon." It was one reason why almost nobody was about. But then the farm folks never come in unless it's Saturday, and the town ladies were home fixing a noonday meal for their families. My father says most weekdays you can shoot a cannon down Main Street and not hit a single living soul.

Truth of the matter is, you'd probably need two cannons 'cause the business section of Jenkinsville is T-shaped. Main Street running up and down and Front Street running crossways. Most of the really important things like our store, the Rice County National Bank, the post office, the picture show, the Sav-Mor Market, and the Victory Cafe are on Main. I passed by the Victory and read the sign painted in neat red lettering at the bottom of the plate-glass window: PLATE LUNCH 25¢. Meat & 3 Vegs.

The smell of fried ham had taken command of the

11

air, so it was impossible to know exactly which three vegetables the Victory was serving.

And there, stuck between the Victory Cafe and the Sav-Mor Market, was our store—best in town. I liked the sign; it's been freshly painted. Big, bold, black letters with a dash of red for emphasis:

BERGEN'S DEPARTMENT STORE
Quality Goods for the Whole Family
Shoes, Clothing, Hardware, & Variety

Standing at the piece-goods counter with my father was a salesman, probably from Memphis or Little Rock, who was removing samples of men's dress shoes from a fitted black case. My father took a package of Tums from his freshly pressed suit coat, and as he popped one into his mouth he nodded at the salesman. "Give me the usual run of sizes in the brogue. Black only."

I wondered if I had time to give my father the news of the prisoners. I mean, if I talked fast. Better to test the water first. "Hello," I said, taking a step forward.

He dropped the Tums back into his pocket. "What are you doing here?"

The salesman smiled at my father. "This your daughter. Harry?"

My father's head moved slightly.

The salesman gave me a full smile. "Well, well, what's your name, sweetheart?"

"Patricia Ann Bergen, sir."

"That's a pretty name for a pretty girl. Here I have something for you." He pulled out a package of Juicy Fruit gum. The wrapper showed the soil of having lived in his pockets for a while.

"Well, thank you anyway, but you see I have this cavity," I lied.

"Oh, that's all right," he said as though he hadn't heard me. "You don't have to chew it now. Take it home."

I took the gum, thanking him as I backed away. I eased my disappointment by telling myself how smart I was to save my story for a more appropriate time.

I looked around for my mother. She was sitting on one of the three cushioned chairs in the shoe department with Gussie Fields, who had been clerking here since even before her husband died.

"Hello," I said, remembering to smile.

My mother said, "Hello," and Mrs. Fields said something about how pretty my dress was.

"She's only wearing that dress because Ruth told her to," my mother said.

"Ruth did *not* tell me to wear this dress," I said, hating the idea of being anybody's robot. Even Ruth's.

"What's Ruth doing?" she asked.

"Washing the clothes." I anticipated the next question so I just supplied the answer. "Sharon is playing in the sandpile."

"Did Ruth give you both lunch?"

"Yes, ma'am."

Mrs. Fields smiled her adult-to-child smile. "How are you enjoying your school vacation? As much as my niece, Donna Ann?"

I wondered how I could honestly answer the question. First I'd have to decide how much I was enjoying the summer—not all that much—then find out exactly how much Donna Ann Rhodes was enjoying it before trying to make an accurate comparison. Mrs. Fields' smile began to fade. Maybe she just wanted me to say something pleasant. "Yes, ma'am," I answered.

"When I was a girl," said my mother, turning toward Mrs. Fields, "I used to drive my mother crazy with my clothes. If my dress wasn't new or if it had the slightest little wrinkle in it I'd cry and throw myself across my bed."

"You were just particular how you looked," said Mrs. Fields.

"I wish Patricia would be more particular," Mother

13

said with sudden force. "Would you just look at that hair?"

"I don't have a comb," I answered.

Reaching into the side pocket of her dress, she produced a small red one. "Here. Go look in the mirror and do a good job. You know, Gussie, you'd expect two sisters to be something alike, but Patricia doesn't care how she looks while Sharon is just like me."

Didn't Mother know I was still standing here? Couldn't she, at the very least, do me the courtesy of talking behind my back? I walked over to the three-way mirror in the dress department, but Mother's voice followed. "Why, before we take the girls to Memphis Sharon has to try on a dozen dresses. And that one? Puts on the first thing her hand touches. She just doesn't care."

I took in my reflection: "Oh, mirror, mirror on the wall, who's the homeliest of them all?"

"Wait till she gets a boyfriend," Mrs. Fields was saying. "She'll spend all her time fixing herself up."

"I wish I was sure of that! Some children just seem to be born with things others aren't. Now, take Sharon, she was never a moment's trouble."

If there were no mirrors or mothers I probably never would know how ugly I am. But it was all there, plain as my reflection in the glass. Skinny bones, skinny face, feet too big, and nose too long. In the mirror I could also see my mother's profile: a high cool forehead and a slender nose that stopped where a nice nose ought to. A lot like Sharon's. And there were the lofty cheekbones that gave mother's face form, symmetry, and on occasion, great beauty. Sometimes I think God lavished so much beauty on her outsides that when he got around to her insides there just wasn't much of anything left over.

When I returned with the comb my mother pulled a stray hair from its teeth before sliding it back into her pocket. "Wonder if Ellie Mae would have time for me?" she said.

Walking to the wall phone, she fluffed her hair into place as she gave the crank a couple of turns. "Mary, please ring up M'Lady Beauty Parlor in Wynne City. . . . No, I don't have the number," she said, resting her arm on the Rice County telephone directory.

"Mother, did you hear about the POWs?" I asked. "A bunch of them just came in by train."

"I don't know why they don't keep them over in Europe where they belong. It's dangerous having those criminals a mile from town." Her head shifted back to the speaker. "Hello, is this Ellie Mae? . . . Do you know who this is? . . . Well, Ellie Mae, I can be in Wynne City in about fifteen minutes. Do you think you could take me right away? . . . Just a wash and set and one of your nice color rinses. . . . Oh, fine, see you in a few minutes."

Actually, and I've told her this, her hair looks its very best just before she goes to the beauty parlor. By the time they finish with her it's tight and unreal, like the hair on a department store manikin.

I watched her tear off a strip of adding-machine tape and write, "$5 Pearl," before exchanging her scribbled note for a fresh five-dollar bill.

As my mother carefully applied her make-up in front of the three-way mirror, Mrs. Burton Benn came into the store looking as though she was on an important mission. A step away from my mother she halted. "Mrs. Bergen," she said, in the same tone that she must use when calling her Sunday-school class together, "I have something to say."

My mother smiled. "What can I do for you today, Mrs. Benn?"

"It's about your Nigra!" said Mrs. Benn.

"Ruth?" answered my mother as though she weren't completely sure of the name.

"Yes, Ruth! After supper last night the Reverend told me that I ought to leave the dishes and get right over to the Sav-Mor Market, take advantage of the marked down hamburg. *Well,"* she said, making the word sound important. "Your Ruth, that uppity Nigra, sees me making a bee-line for the meat counter and she practically breaks out in a run to get there first. She tells Gene, 'Give me the rest of that hamburg.'" Mrs. Benn's voice sounded like a white woman trying to imitate a colored one. "Now, you just tell me what's a darky gonna do with two pounds of hamburg? All she wanted was to keep me from getting any and that's the truth!"

"Oh," said my mother, sounding genuinely grieved. "She's probably eaten it by now."

"I don't *want* that meat!"

"What do you want?" asked my mother, confused.

"To teach her a lesson. I want you to fire her!"

I watched my mother gently shake her head No. She's getting ready to tell off Mrs. Benn, I thought. She's going to tell her how good and kind Ruth is—how much we love her, Sharon and me. "I just can't fire Ruth," she apologized. "She's the best cook and house cleaner we've ever had."

In the shoe department my father sat alone, his lean body half-hidden behind the open pages of the afternoon *Memphis Press Scimitar.*

"I came here specially to tell you," I began, wishing that Ruth could hear all my sweetness, "about the Nazis that came into Jenkinsville on the eleven thirty train."

He turned from the paper. "What about them?"

I felt like an actress who finally gets her big chance, but just at the moment the spotlights expose her she remembers that she has neglected to learn her lines. "Well," I said, "there was a whole bunch of them. They were about as big and mean-looking as anybody could be."

His eyes went back to the *Press Scimitar.*

"Well, aren't you interested in the really exciting thing that happened?"

16

"What happened?"

Some people say that God strikes down a liar—
Boom! I decided to risk it. "One of the prisoners tried
to escape."

A wrinkle of genuine interest came slicing between
his neat black eyebrows. "You mean, after they got off
the train?"

"Yes, sir. As soon as he stepped off the train, I
noticed that his head started moving around, so right
away I became suspicious. I guess the guard noticed it
too because he came right up behind him and said,
'Make one move and I'll blow your brains out.' Just like
that. 'I'll blow your brains out.' "

"Is that all?"

"Yes, sir, that's all."

"Then let me read my paper in peace."

If you follow Main past Front Street, the road con-
tinues even though the pavement ends. I stood at the
corner looking down the narrow dirt road towards Nigger Bottoms, wishing to be black for a while so that I
could enter into the other Jenkinsville. By the side of
the road two women stood. Nearby, a scrawny rooster
chased a large speckled hen. The bigger of the women
pointed to the hysterical hen before leaning her head
close to the ear of her friend. Suddenly their heads fell
back and the high notes of their laughter carried all the
way up to Front Street.

The thought came to me that even from a distance
people dislike being watched. I moved on down Front
Street to Mr. Matthew Hawkes's run-down drugstore.
People say the aspirin old Matty sells has been on the
shelf so long that it gives more headaches than it could
ever take away.

Next to Hawkes's drugstore is Cook Brothers'
Furniture and Appliances. Then comes a secondhand-
clothing store which never had a sign saying what its
name is. After that is Mr. J.G. Jackson's cotton gin

17

office, and the office and printing press of Mr. Quentin Blakey's *Rice County Gazette*.

And right next to the *Gazette*'s office is something interesting. I mean, you wouldn't exactly think it was interesting because there's nothing there now besides a vacant building with a Coca-Cola advertisement and a sign that says THE CHU LEE GROCERY CO. Well, Mr. Lee—everybody called him "the Chink"—was the first merchant to open every morning and the very last to close. Maybe that was because of him and Mrs. Lee living in the back of the store, so convenient and all.

What happened I don't exactly understand. One day he was doing business just like always, and the next day without so much as a going-out-of-business sale he had taken his groceries and left. I guess it happens; people get sick or find better opportunities elsewhere.

But why would there be this hole. bigger than a football, right through the plate-glass window? At first I thought maybe the moving men hadn't been careful when they were carting things out, but when I looked inside the empty store there was all this glass lying around the floor, so the window just had to be broken from the outside.

I would have forgotten all about it except for what I happened to hear Mr. J.G. Jackson say to my father. "Our boys at Pearl Harbor would have got a lot of laughs at the farewell party we gave the Chink." Then Mr. Jackson laughed and my father gave a weak laugh, too, as though his heart wasn't really in it but still he wanted to keep the respect of so important a man as Mr. J.G. Jackson.

Later, when I asked my father what Mr. Jackson meant by that, he told me that I was never in my life to mention it again. All I know is that if Mr. Lee had been Japanese, then it might have made more sense. Anyway, there's probably a simple logical explanation. It couldn't be what I think.

2

IT WAS TEN O'CLOCK Sunday morning when my father came back from doing his bookwork at the store and asked, just as nice as you please, if we were all ready to go to Memphis. Like he didn't mind at all. My mother dearly loves "to go home" again. And Sharon likes playing with our little cousins, Diane and Jerry. Me? Sometimes Grandpa and I discuss the important things that are happening in the world. We both, for example, think President Roosevelt is a very great man. I talk a lot with Grandma too, but she's always asking me questions: Am I gaining any weight?—not really. How am I doing at school?—I make a lot of Cs. Then she gets around to the hardest question of all: Do I have a lot of friends?—I guess so.

But even with the questions Grandma and Grandpa are nice, so I've never understood exactly why my father disliked them so much.

I think the problem may have started when he married my mother, and Grandpa didn't give him a job in his real estate business, S. Fried & Sons. Now, my father is always saying that he'd rather starve than have to work for Grandpa and his brothers-in-law, but I think he resented it all the same. Because the company is big enough not only for Grandpa and his two sons but for two of Grandpa's nephews and even the outsider, Bernard Kaplan, who runs the insurance end of things.

Considering the trouble my father had with his own parents, it's really sad that he doesn't have in-laws he can love. Even now, he never ever mentions his own mother. I don't remember Grandma Bergen as being mean, but I was only about Sharon's age when she died, so I don't know for sure. About the only sure thing I remember is her hair, which was auburn like mine. And I'm not the only one who's noticed that. Uncle Max, my father's oldest brother, says my hair, my eyes, and even "my way" remind him of her.

Uncle Max also told me that on a poor working-class street like Hamel Street, in South Memphis, the Bergens were considered the poorest of the poor. Grandma Bergen's dresses were washed so many times that the threads were almost countable. And poor Grandpa Bergen, a cobbler, died of a heart attack at forty-two when he was only seven dollars short of saving enough for a stitching machine. With one of those machines he was sure he could repair enough shoes to support his family.

Which gets to another point. Since the Bergens were so poor, I think my father would still be a ticket seller at Union Station if it hadn't been for Grandpa and Grandma Fried's lending him the money to go into business. So wouldn't you expect him to be all choked up with gratitude? Well, he's not! Maybe it's because he hates favors—not so much to give as to take them. "I don't like to be obligated," is the way he puts it. It's as though, in his own heart, he believes that he could never have made it without them. And he hates having needed them. But that doesn't make a lot of sense.

"Lock the doors," my father ordered as he backed the car down the driveway. At the First Baptist Church corner I touched his shoulder and pointed towards the glass-enclosed sign in the churchyard. "Hey, did you see that? It says, 'Sin now—pay later.' I didn't know they charged for that, did you?" I started up a laugh, but when nobody joined in, it made a hollow sound.

"O.K.," he said, "don't bother me when I'm driving."

Suddenly Sharon jumped off the back seat and touched my father's shoulder at the very spot I had touched. "There's a bee on you!" she shouted. "April fools!"

From deep within his throat my father chuckled, while Mother turned around to give Sharon a love pinch on her cheek. "Are you the bad girl that fooled your daddy?" she asked.

Sharon reached out to touch the neck of Mother's lavender dress. "There's a bee on you. April fools!" She squealed with delight.

Mother pretended horror. "Get that bee away!" she said, swatting at the neck of her dress.

After a few more of Sharon's April-fool bees, Mother seemed to tire of the game. "Can't you do something?" she asked me. "Amuse Sharon. Tell her the story of the 'Three Little Pigs.' "

"I don't know if I remember that story," I lied. "But the story of 'Cinderella' and her wicked stepmother is still fresh in my mind."

At the end of the story when Cinderella marries the world's handsomest prince at the world's fanciest wedding Sharon sighed, looking every bit as happy as the bride and a whole lot sleepier. She curled up in the corner, and with just a touch of a smile on her lips, fell asleep.

"So, if we take the men's underwear to the back of the store," Mother was saying, "we could use the front counter for an impulse item."

"Men's underwear is a big seller. We sold more than six thousand dollars' worth last year."

"But, Harry, we'd sell every bit as much," she argued, "because men come in specially to buy it. But with women's blouses it's different. A woman sees something pretty and she just ups and buys it spur of the moment."

"Well," said my father as though he didn't want to give in too quickly, "don't go moving things tomorrow; we've got a lot of merchandise waiting to be checked in."

When we reached the two-lane Harrihan Bridge that connects West Memphis, Arkansas, to Memphis, Tennessee, I looked down at the bluey-brown Mississippi. They say the river's current is strong and very few people have ever been able to swim across, although not a year goes by that somebody doesn't drown in the attempt. This may sound crazy because the only time I ever go swimming is a couple of times in early summer when Edna Louise Jackson's mother takes a bunch of us to the public pool in Wynne City, but I could swim it. The secret is in absolutely refusing to let the river beat you down. If I had to, I'd measure my progress in inches. One more inch I've swum—one less inch to swim. Once you know the secret, then nobody's river can bring you down.

On Riverside Drive, "Memphis's front door," my father dropped his speed down to between thirty and thirty-five miles per hour.

My mother was resting her head against the seat, her eyes closed as though she were dozing. She was wearing her healthy-looking black hair in my favorite way—brushed back so that her widow's peak shone like an extra added attraction above her high forehead. And hers wasn't an everyday pretty face. The shape of the nose, the cut of the chin, but it was more than that—more than its parts. My mother's face was an artist's vision of sensitivity, intelligence, and love. And so it had to be a big lie what they say about beauty being only skin deep. For if it weren't really there why would it show?

The problem must be me. I've never been what she wanted, never done what she asked. Always making my own little changes and additions. Why do I do it? Why can't I be better? More obedient? More loving?

22

I leaned over, placing my lips against hers. Those lips suddenly tightened. And there I stood, still bending over her. Ugly, naked, and alone.

She opened her eyes. "I wish you wouldn't bother me when I'm trying to sleep."

"Sorry," I answered, letting my head fall against the window of the back seat.

"I've been meaning to tell you," she said after a short period of quiet. "If Grandmother tries to give you money you just tell her you don't need anything."

"But I do need something," I answered, wondering if she could understand.

She didn't answer. She put her head back against the seat and closed her eyes again.

"If I were a rich grandmother with plenty of money," I said, "I would enjoy giving things to my grandchildren." I touched her shoulder. "Could you please tell me why it's all right for you to take things from Grandma—the mink coat, for example."

Her eyes shot open. "That was my birthday present."

At least I had her attention. "Well, then what about all that new porch furniture? That wasn't anybody's birthday present."

"That was an anniversary present—for being married to your daddy for fourteen years."

That wasn't a present, I thought, more a reward. I couldn't, at the moment, decide which one deserved the reward. Neither. Both. The only thing I could think to say was, "Oh." Until a few moments later I thought of something else. "What if Grandma has money for Sharon. Is that O.K.?"

"Sharon's little," she answered.

My father followed Jackson Avenue eastward until he came to the old stone gates of Hein Park, mostly hidden now by a pair of weeping willows. Grandpa had told me of last winter's ice storm, and how the elms and maples had been damaged. Only the willows

23

remained intact. "Bending," he had said, "beats breaking."

Hein Park was the greenest and most elegant residential area in the whole city. It had narrow, leafy roads which wound past fine old homes set back on limey green grass.

I nudged Sharon. "Hey, sleepyhead, wake up." She looked at me reproachfully, like Cinderella being disturbed while waltzing with the prince. "Come on, we're almost there." Her expression didn't change for the better, but she did manage to lift her chin as I retied the ribbon bow at her neck.

And there it was—my grandparents' house. A twelve-room Victorian painted the whitest white with windows large enough to welcome in the sun, each with its green-and-white-striped awning sloping down like a circus tent. It would have been nice growing up in that house.

Before we reached the front steps Grandpa was already at the door. He turned to shout over his shoulder, "Mamma, they're here! Pearl and Harry."

Grandpa has every bit as much hair today as he did in the wedding picture that sits on his bedroom bureau. Now, forty years later, it has changed color, and so has his expression. Then it was—resolute. Yes, resolute. And now it's just gentle.

His freshly shaved face carried the aroma of Old Spice. "My oldest grandchild—already a young lady," he said, hugging and kissing me.

From the kitchen, the warm, sweet smell of cooking—of roast turkey and carrot *tsimmes*.

"How are you, Boss-man?" my father asked, without shaking hands. "Tell me when you poor folks here in Hein Park are going to be able to afford some sidewalks." It was his favorite joke.

Grandpa said, "Soon as my rich son-in-law lends me the money," which happened to be his favorite answer.

24

Grandma came from the kitchen, wiping her hands on her flowery apron. Through the years Grandma has put on weight and now her face, while not exactly a perfect circle, is all the same quite round. Last time we were visiting, Grandpa said that he married a 90-pound girl and now he's got a 180-pound woman. Twice what he bargained for. That was about the only time I ever saw her mad. She insisted that she didn't weigh an ounce over 165.

Grandma hugged and kissed us all, with the exception of my father who hurriedly brushed past her on his way to the big chair with the matching ottoman.

Then she started worrying whether or not we were hungry. Uncle Ben and Uncle Irv weren't coming for another hour and a half, about two o'clock. "Pearl, wouldn't you like a nice bowl of soup now? Maybe Harry and the children would like a little something to hold them."

"Oh, Mother, I hope you didn't cook one of your big starchy dinners. You know I have to watch my weight."

"Watch your weight at your own house. Here, when my children and grandchildren come to visit, I cook."

Mother agreed to a cup of coffee, and my father, after finding out that it was chicken soup with matzo balls, his favorite, relented.

"I saw your brother, Max," Grandpa said to my father. "He doesn't go to many of the brotherhood meetings. He's a nice fellow, your brother."

"Good as gold," my father agreed. "And if you ever want the world to know something, just tell him. Worst blabbermouth in town."

Grandpa let his lips pout forward as if the thought were new and surprising. "I should worry about that? I'm too old for women. I pay my bills. I never hurt anybody. People with dark secrets should worry about Max. Me? I'm not going to worry."

Actually, Uncle Max wasn't really so much of a blabbermouth as he was a rememberer. There wasn't much that he forgot about people, especially about his family. I think that's why my father always seems funny—a little tense—around him. Maybe he enjoys remembering what my father enjoys forgetting.

Like the time last Yom Kippur when we were all standing around outside the Beth Zion Synagogue and one of Uncle Max's remembrances made my father so angry that he called him, "A damn liar," right to his face. He was telling what a hot temper my father had had when he was a boy. How he sometimes became uncontrollably mad at one of his brothers, usually Arnie. More than once, according to Uncle Max, Grandfather Bergen had to sit on his son's bed late at night, repeating, "You will not be violent. You will not be violent!"

Grandpa sat down next to me on the gold brocade sofa. "You been writing any more letters to the editor of the *Commercial Appeal?*" he asked, patting my arm.

"Oh, no, sir, not any more. I only wrote that one because of that stupid man who wrote that the war was all President Roosevelt's fault."

"Such an intelligent letter," said Grandpa, adjusting his eyeglasses. "Most people twice your age wouldn't have written so well."

I turned my head to see what my father thought of that. But he was too deep into *Look* magazine's story about a soldier's farewell to hear. And my mother was only interested in her fingernails, which she was filing with a well-used emery board. For a moment I thought I might come right out and ask her if she had liked my letter too, but I didn't. I didn't want to give her the impression that her opinion was all that important to me.

The dining room table was set for fourteen with a fine damask cloth, sterling-silver flatware, and real crystal glasses, two for each setting. Grandma always served

26

Mogen David and I couldn't remember a time when I was too young for my own wine glass. I could always tell how grown-up Grandma considered me by how much wine she poured. When I was Sharon's age only the bottom of the glass was covered, but when I was ten it was at the halfway mark. Last Chanukah, and I'm not exaggerating, it was three-quarters.

At our house we have damask cloths, crystal, and sterling too, but I can't remember my mother ever using them. Anyway, I know she's never cooked a dinner like Grandma. Now, Ruth is a very good cook too, but it's not the same. It's still like eating somebody else's food, while Grandma's is like finally coming home.

On the gas stove were two restaurant-sized pots, one filled with simmering golden soup and the other had kasha with noodle bows. Grandma opened the door of the oven, slid out the rack, and basted the turkey with a large metal spoon. She wiped her hands on a kitchen towel before looking me over. "My grandchildren are growing up," she said, sighing. "And when do I see you? Why don't you like visiting your grandmother?"

"But I do!"

"I ask your mother why she never brings you on the train with her, she says you're too busy with all your friends."

"My mother told you that?" I asked, not believing.

"Your mother always tells me that," she anwered.

"Well, she's telling a lie."

Grandma looked at me and then she nodded her head as if she knew just what to do about it. "Listen, next week we'll plan a day; you take the eight o'clock morning train and we'll spend the whole day together. I'll buy you clothes—anything you want. We'll have lunch together. You like the top of the Hotel Peabody, the Skyway?"

"I just love it!" I said. "I've never been there but

sometimes I listen to WREC; they broadcast the dinner music right from the Skyway. I've always wanted to go there. Will Mother go too?"

"Well," said Grandma, thinking it over. Suddenly she shook her head No. "Let her stay home. She'll only tell me you don't need a thing and somehow we'll end up shopping for her."

"I can't wait," I said, feeling as though she had slipped into my team's colors. Backtracking, I tried to remember exactly what it was Grandma had said about buying me anything I wanted. Did that mean only clothes?

"Is there something wrong?"

"Oh, no, ma'am," I said, knowing it was those two vertical think-lines that sometimes invite themselves to my forehead that prompted her question. "It's just that I was wondering if—I mean, if I don't buy but one dress and if it's not too expensive do you think it might be all right if I bought a book? You see, we don't have a library in town except for the one at school and that's closed for the summer."

Suddenly she held up her index finger. "Wait!" she ordered, leaving the room in a rush. When she returned, she was folding a ten-dollar bill in half. "Take this," she said, "and buy some nice books and when you finish reading them, I'll give you money to buy more."

Stepping backward I clasped my hands behind my back. I tried to remember why I wasn't supposed to take the money. "Well, thanks anyway but—"

She pulled my arm from behind my back and systematically opened my fingers one by one to place the bill in my palm. "Buy what makes you happy," said Grandma.

"But my mother said—"

"Your mother!" A deep crease appeared on one side of her mouth. "This is not for your mother to know!"

28

Grandma poured my mother's coffee and set it down on the kitchen table along with a cup of matzo-ball soup for Sharon. Then she took a large blue crockery bowl and carefully ladled in the steaming broth before dropping in two fat matzo balls. At the kitchen door she called out, "Soup's ready." My father came at once, sat down, and finished off his soup while Sharon was still blowing on maybe the second or third spoonful.

My mother set her coffee cup down and asked, "How is it, Harry?"

"Not bad," he said, accepting his second bowl.

When I heard car doors slamming I looked at the kitchen clock—ten minutes after two. My little cousins, Diane and Jerry, were the first to run in. As I kissed Uncle Irv I saw that everybody else had found somebody to kiss. Uncle Ben called my mother "Sis" and asked, "How's everything?"

Then I heard Aunt Dorothy laughing her high-pitched laugh. "Don't kiss me, Harry. I might swoon."

"Come here, you beautiful thing, and kiss a real man," said my father, "and you'll never go back to that husband of yours."

Now it so happens Aunt Dorothy is no beautiful thing. Frankly speaking, she has buck teeth and good-sized pits on her cheeks, left over from her acne years. And her figure is fatless, though certainly not faultless. Sort of muscle and bone under tightly stretched skin, probably because of all the golf she plays. Two or three years ago her picture was in the *Commercial Appeal* when she won the Ridgeway Country Club's women's golf championship.

My father led Aunt Dorothy to the window side of the living room and began whispering in her ear. Suddenly her head fell back and she laughed like a woman laughs who wants to please a man. "Oh, Harry, you're a real card," she said.

29

It has always seemed strange to me, but women like my father. Of course, he's forever giving them attention, telling them what a big deal they are, so beautiful and all. My Uncle Max told me that my father was the only one of the five Bergen boys who was a genuine "ladies' man," spending his pay on clothes and girls. I thought he was just fooling me, but later I asked Aunt Rose which one of her brothers was the most popular with the girls, and right off the bat she answered, "Your daddy. The girls were crazy about him." But he can be very nice to other people. I've noticed that.

When we all sat down at the dining room table, each place had its own small plate of chopped liver resting on a leaf of lettuce. Grandpa stood and raised his wine glass. I reached for mine, and for the first time it was completely full. Just as full as Grandpa's or Uncle Ben's and if I'm not mistaken it was slightly fuller than my mother's.

At the moment of absolute quiet, Grandpa spoke. "We pray that we'll all be together for many, many years to come. And that Hitler and his Nazis should be finished—*Kaput!* And our dear President Roosevelt should be given a long life and much wisdom. *L'chayim!*"

"*L'chayim,*" we repeated, bringing our glasses to our lips.

The talk centered on war news. The fate of the Jews, the capture of General Wainright, and the Russian offensive on the Kalinin Front. My father gave dire warnings about the Russians—how it would be better if they were fighting against us. That way we could destroy both Hitler and Stalin at the same time. Two birds with one stone.

"Why do we always talk war, war, war?" my mother finally asked. "Why don't we ever talk about happy things like clothes or parties? Something nice?"

Aunt Dorothy nodded in agreement. "Ben, tell

your sister about the insurance meeting in New York that the company is sending us all to."

"Irv and I want to take in all the sights," said Uncle Ben. "But all the girls can talk about is shopping and plays. Plays and shopping!"

My mother turned her gaze from Uncle Ben to my grandfather. "You're sending them on a vacation but not me?"

Grandpa shook his head. "I'm not sending them any place—the company is."

"Papa, you *are* the company!" said my mother, not hiding the anger in her voice. "And you've always done that, given everything to your precious boys. Don't I count for anything? Don't I deserve something nice too?"

My grandma's chin lifted as though it had been struck by an uppercut. "That's foolish talk, Pearl. Foolish! The difference between you and your brothers is that they always liked whatever they were given, but you, Pearl, never liked anything once it was yours."

It was early evening when we drove across the Harrihan Bridge, entering the neon strip of highways known as West Memphis, Arkansas.

I leaned back into my dark corner of the car, patted my skirt pocket, and felt reassured by the folded square of paper. Grandma's ten-dollar bill. On the seat next to me was a whole bag of her freshly made cheese and onion *knishes*. I breathed in deep. It was as though I had just left home and was now going to where I lived.

3

WALKING BACK DOWN Main Street with the bank bag heavy with rolls of dimes, quarters, and halves, I began wondering what I could do with the rest of this Monday. If only I lived in Wynne City, there'd be no problem. The public pool is filled with kids, more kids than chlorine; the school library is open even when school isn't; and the Capitol Theater has a matinee practically every afternoon.

A drab-olive truck, canvas-covered from top to sides, passed. I recognized it as the Army truck that had picked up the prisoners from the train station. It turned and angle-parked in front of our store.

Two men in Army uniform and wearing guns in polished leather holsters jumped from the cab. One of the soldiers, quite muscular despite a prominent belly, called to the back of the truck, "All right, out! Everybody out."

And out they came: young men. Two, three, four. Not much older than boys. Five, six, seven. Wearing their matched sets of blue denims. Eight, nine, and ten. As they walked towards the entrance of the store the backs of their shirts revealed for all the world to see the stenciled black letters: POW.

They were, with one exception, blond- or brown-haired and wore pleasant enough expressions. Didn't they know they were losing the war? That they were at this moment entering a Jewish store?

As I followed the last prisoner inside, I watched my father approach the guard with the corporal's stripes. "Something I can do for you boys today?"

"Yes, sir, Mr. Bergen. These prisoners been spending more time passing out in Mr. Jackson's field than they do picking cotton. So Mr. Jackson gave them two dollars apiece and the commandant said it was all right to bring them here for field hats." He pointed toward the one black-haired prisoner who was moving away from the herd. "Reiker there speaks American. He'll talk for them."

"Tell the boys to come over to the hat department," my father said as though he didn't hate them. As if he had never said, "Every German oughta be taken out and tortured to death."

When the nine prisoners were gathered around the counter the corporal shouted, "Reiker!" Reiker didn't look quite so tall or strong as the others. His eyes, specked with green, sought communication with my father. "The men wish to purchase straw field hats to protect themselves from your formidable Arkansas sun."

My father remained impassive. "Here are some styles in men's straws. These are the best quality at one dollar and seventy-nine cents. They will last you for years."

Last you for years? I checked out my father's face to see if he was making a joke at their expense. But it was empty of expression.

The Germans began trying on the hats, smiling as though they were on a holiday. Reiker had pushed out from the center huddle and was exploring the broader limits of the store.

One very blond prisoner turned to my father. *"Der Spiegel?"*

33

My father shook his head. "I don't know what you're talking about."

"*Wo ist der Spiegel?*" said a second prisoner.

Again my father shook his head. "I don't understand your talk!"

Voices called for Reiker, and at his approach the men parted like the Red Sea for the Israelites. Again the word "*Spiegel.*" Reiker turned to my father. "They'd like to see themselves. Have you a mirror?"

Reiker used English cleanly, easily, and with more precision than anyone I know from around these parts. And he didn't sound the least bit like a German. It was as though he had spent his life learning to speak English the way the English do.

Again Reiker left the others to walk with brisk steps across the store.

The corporal was involved in selecting off-duty socks for himself while the other guard leaned heavily against a counter and rolled himself a cigarette. Neither seemed concerned as Reiker headed unobserved towards the door. He could be gone before they even got their guns out of their holsters. Terrified that the guards' casualness was only a cover for the sharpest-shooting soldiers in anybody's army, I closed my eyes and prayed that he would make it all the way to freedom.

But I heard no door opening, no feet running, and no gun firing. By sheer force of will I opened my eyes to see Reiker calmly examining the pencils at the stationery counter.

Stationery was one of the many departments seen to by Sister Parker. But Sister Parker was busy waiting on a lady customer, and lady customers take half of forever to make up their minds. Who was going to wait on Reiker? I wanted to, but I couldn't. I didn't even have a comb. Why, in God's name, didn't I carry a purse with a fresh handkerchief and a comb like Edna Louise? I ran my fingers through my hair and patted it into place.

34

I took a few hurried steps and stopped short. Reiker may not wish to be disturbed, anyway not by me. The skin-and-bones girl. But I can wait on him if I want to, it's my father's store. Who does he think he is, some old Nazi?

Pushed on by adrenalin, I was at his side. "Could I help you, please?" My voice came out phony. Imitation Joan Crawford.

Reiker looked up and smiled. "Yes, please. I don't know the word for it—" Above those eyes with their specks of green were dark masculine eyebrows. "Pocket pencil sharpeners? They're quite small and work on the razor principle."

"Well," I said, reaching towards the opposite end of the counter to pick up a little red sharpener, "we sell a lot of these dime ones to the school children."

"Yes," he said. "Exactly right." He was looking at me like he saw me—like he liked what he saw.

"What color would you like?" I asked, not really thinking about pencil sharpeners. "They come in red, yellow, and green."

"I'll take the one you chose," said Reiker. He placed six yellow pencils and three stenographic pads on the counter. "And you did not tell me," he said, "what you call these pocket pencil sharpeners."

He was so nice. How could he have been one of those—those brutal, black-booted Nazis? "Well, I don't think they actually call them much of anything, but if they were to call them by their right name they'd probably call them pocket pencil sharpeners."

Reiker laughed and for a moment, this moment, we were friends. And now I knew something more. He wasn't a bad man.

"Could I ask you something?" I asked, impressed by my own nerve. His face registered the kind of flat openness that comes when you haven't the slightest idea what to expect. "Well, I was wondering how—where you learned to speak such good English?"

35

He seemed relieved. "No great credit to me." He showed fine, white teeth. "My mother was born in Manchester, in England, and my father was educated in London."

"Gee, that's something," I said, immediately regretting my "gee." "Being born in one country," I went on, "and then having to go clear over to another to get educated."

"Keep in mind the relative smallness of European countries. It's like being born in Arkansas and going to a university in, say, Tennessee."

"Oh," I answered, still feeling the grandeur of it. "What did he study in England?"

"History. He's an historian."

"I never met an historian. What do they do? Teach?"

"What is your name?" he asked, quietly.

"Well, my real name is Patricia Ann Bergen," I said, grateful that I was able to remember. "Mostly, though, my friends call me Patty."

"And my real name is Frederick Anton Reiker, and when I had friends they always called me Anton. So I hope you will too, Patty."

"O.K.," I said, feeling too shy to speak his name.

"Back to your questions." He sounded very businesslike. "My father is a professor at the University of Göttingen in Germany. Before the war he wrote two books and a great many articles, but not any more. Now nobody is allowed to write." Anton sighed as though he had just run out of energy.

"And did you teach too?" I asked, wanting to know everything there was to know about him.

Anton moved his head from side to side. "Before I became a cotton picker I was a private in the German Army and before that a medical student."

"Someday when the war is over," I heard the sound of conviction in my voice, "you'll go back to school, become a doctor."

Anton shrugged. "Someday—perhaps." Then with a grin calculated to banish heaviness he said, "I believe it's here in the cotton fields of Arkansas that I'm destined to find fame and fortune." My smile joined his.

"Yes," I agreed. "You and Mr. Eli Whitney."

"Eli Whitney?" Anton repeated. "Should I know him?"

I searched his face for fraud. Surely a man as smart as he would know what every third-grader knows. "Well, Eli Whitney invented the cotton gin; it sucks all the seeds out of cotton like a giant vacuum cleaner."

"Clever of Mr. Whitney. Perhaps even genius. What is genius, anyway, if it isn't the ability to give an adequate response to a great challenge?"

"I don't know" I said thoughtfully. "I'll have to think about that."

"I hope you do, Patty. Next time we meet you can tell me your conclusions."

A distant voice intruded upon us. "All right, boys, the truck is leaving. Let's go."

Anton took a dollar bill from a cocoa-brown wallet made of the smoothest calfskin. A fine wallet, better even than our very best ones and they sell for five dollars. I counted back the change.

"Good-bye, Patty."

"Good-bye, Anton. I hope you'll be all right."

As he turned to go, my eyes closed. I found myself carrying on a silent conversation with God. Oh, God, would it be at all possible for Frederick Anton Reiker to become my friend? I understand that it's not an easy request, but I would be so grateful that I'd never bother you for another thing. But if this is something you can't arrange, then could you please keep him safe so that he can return to his own country and become a doctor? Thank you, dear God.

"Patty!" Anton's voice. I opened my eyes. He was pointing to some object behind the glass-enclosed jewelry counter. "Sell me this pin. The round one in back that looks like diamonds."

I followed his pointing finger. It was big and gaudy, nothing that Anton would in a million years buy. "Not this one?" I asked, expecting to be embarrassed by so obvious a mistake.

"Exactly right!" he practically shouted, as he took the pin tagged a dollar, dropped the money into my hand, and went off grinning a different, more jaunty kind of grin. — prediction —

4

SISTER PARKER HELD the canvas bank bag aloft. "Patty, you know anything about this? Found it lying on the stationery counter."

"Oh! Yes, thanks. Change from the bank."

"Don't you know any better than to leave a bag of money lying around?"

"I was waiting on a customer and I forgot. Uh, don't mention it, please, to my mother or father."

Sister shook her head. "I've got better things to do than tattle."

I found my mother between dress racks with one of those heavy, colorless country women who all look alike until you focus in on the one thing that gives them their uniqueness. Sometimes it's the forehead that gives a faint suggestion of things noble. Once, I remember, it was long polished hair of deepest auburn. And another time it was the eyes. Large blue-green eyes that seemed to have come from the sockets of some jungle cat.

I lifted the bank bag to eye level. "Here's your change, Mother."

"Go put it in the big register. Where have you been so long?"

"Well, I just finished waiting on one of the prisoners and before that I stopped to talk with Edna Louise's mother—she was in the bank too."

"I didn't know," said my mother, "that you and

39

Mrs. Jackson had anything in common." She made an adjustment of the three-way mirror, presumably to give the customer a better view of her large economy-size behind.

I felt angry enough to burn my mother in her own insult, but open anger was not the tool I needed. "Know what Mrs. Jackson said to me? She said, 'Patty, it's always a deep and abiding pleasure talking with you.' Then she asked me, know what she asked me?" I could see that Mother wasn't going to bite, so I went right on. " 'Patty,' Mrs. Jackson said, 'just tell me where in this wide world did you acquire those nice, polite manners?' "

Mother glanced at me, shivering as if from a sudden chill. "Can't you do anything about that hair?" Then she turned back to her customer with a smile. "Now that fabric is what we call a bemberg sheer. It's lightweight, easy to care for, and very cool and comfortable. And I do believe that rose is your color, don't you think so? Do you know how much you'd have to pay for that dress in Memphis?" Mother apparently assumed that Mrs. Country Woman didn't know the answer, so she supplied it. "Ten ninety-five and not a penny less. But we only have a few left, and I'm closing them out at only five ninety-five."

Mother is what you might call a prize saleslady. I mean, she has an answer for everything. If there were silver-dollar-sized holes running across the backside of that dress Mother would be talking about how fine it is for ventilation, or maybe even that it was a definite aid for irregularity.

Now, customers expect salesladies to praise the merchandise, that's only natural. But I don't believe you should outright lie. God would consider that sinful even for a saleslady. But then, what would God think about the lies I tell—"Where in this wide world did you acquire those nice, polite manners?"

I punched the No Sale key on the register and

40

placed the rolls of change into their appropriate bins. I watched my mother still smiling her gracious smile as she set a pink leftover Easter bonnet on the woman's head. "Now doesn't that just make the outfit?"

Mrs. Country Woman shook her head. "No, ma'am, I don't want no hat today."

"That's perfectly all right," Mother said, soothingly. "I just wanted you to see the big difference the hat makes."

The woman pushed a loose straggle of hair beneath the bonnet and gave herself a front-view inspection. I thought I saw her smile. Yes, she had found something in her reflection to admire. She would buy the hat too; my mother would see to that.

But I didn't want to think about leftover bonnets or even my mother's ability as a saleslady. I only wanted to think about him. My friend, Anton. "The next time we meet," he had said. Anton Reiker. Mr. Frederick Anton Reiker.

Across the store, in Notions, Sister Parker was customerless, but far from idle. What is it I've heard Ruth say about idle hands and the devil? Sister Parker has no worries on that score. Her left hand held a couple of bottles of lotion while the right hand gave them a dusting with a big wad of cheesecloth.

Maybe it would be O.K. to talk to her about him, but not exactly straight off. First I'd talk about the prisoners in general. Later I might just mention that Anton didn't seem too bad—for a German. But I would approach with caution. Her kid brother, James Earl, will probably be sent to fight the Germans just as soon as he finishes up his basic training.

I stood by her side and tried to come up with a good opening. "Hey, that was pretty interesting wasn't it? All those Germans coming in here buying things."

Sister Parker's hands didn't stop for a single moment. "I don't see much interesting about a bunch of Nazis." Her answers, like her hands, moved quickly. It

41

was as though she kept them on the topmost part of her brain for easy access.

"Well, I think it's interesting," I countered. "Gives you a chance to see the enemy close-up."

"I guess," said Sister, unconvinced.

"I wonder why they decided to build a prison camp right outside of Jenkinsville?"

"Well, we have as much empty space around us as anybody else." She sounded pleased with her logic.

"But they have even more empty space in Texas," I said. "Thousands of miles of empty space."

She sighed. Boredom or anger? I don't actually mean to be rude, but I am. My father says I ask a lot of questions and then go around contradicting every answer.

"You're probably right," I said, trying to make amends. "But I wonder who decided that Jenkinsville, Arkansas, would be a good place?"

"The President."

"Oh, not the President! He's much too busy for—" There I go again, contradicting. "Well, I guess it could be that way. Maybe he did have a little free time one day and said, 'Eleanor, I've been thinking about where we could build the new prisoner-of-war camp. In the Arkansas Delta there's a little town called Jenkinsville that would be just perfect. There are fields of cotton needing picking, plenty of open space, and no big city nearby where a prisoner could hide. Yes, Eleanor, Jenkinsville would be ideal.' "

"I guess it could have been decided like that," she said.

I continued to stand there watching the notions counter grow cleaner and more organized. Inside I felt a rising sense of discomfort. I just had to speak of him, of Anton.

I said, "I'll tell you something interesting." Sister glanced at me and I took it to be a go-ahead. "I sold one of the prisoners some pencils and things. He spoke

42

the most perfect English I've ever heard and he was really very polite. I mean, for a German he wasn't half bad."

Sister looked at me more carefully, her hands motionless. Something a little scary about those now-unmoving hands. "I saw you with him. Smiling and laughing. Did you like him?"

Betrayed! By whom? Anton? No, by myself. By my ugly, stupid self. Always having to talk, always having to tell people things.

Not one tear is going to come out of my eye. Strike back. "Sister, if you really want to you can tell everybody in town that lie. I really don't care." Make it good. Make it very, very good. "And I don't know if I should tell you the truth because I'm not certain you deserve it, but I'll tell you anyway. That prisoner was telling me that he hated Hitler more than anybody in this whole world because it was Hitler who had his mother and father killed—and his sister Nancy. And he told me that every night he prayed only one prayer, that God should allow the Americans to win the war."

The cheesecloth flew back into action. "Well, how was I to *know* he told you that?"

"You could have asked," I said, listening to the sounds of injury in my voice. "All you really had to do was ask."

Outside the store the sun had positioned itself in the dead center of the sky. As I walked down the only residential block in town it followed my steps, evaporating my energies. Soon there would be a real (just like the city) street sign on this corner. At the moment, though, nobody knew just what the sign would read. The town ladies, mostly from the missionary society, were holding out for Silk Stocking Street. "Elegant," they said. While Mayor Crawford called it, "A damn silly name."

Actually, there didn't seem to be much need either

for a street name or a sign. Everybody knows where everybody else lives. And if you're worrying about a stranger coming into town. well all he'd have to do is ask. People in this town are friendly and that's the truth.

Set back against freshly mowed grass and twin dogwoods the Jackson house was the only two-story in town. I pressed the doorbell which activated a series of chimes. Always at this point I'd get to feeling foolish. It was too grand a way to announce my arrival. I tried to tell myself that Edna Louise would be glad to see me especially if she didn't have any other visitors. After all, any company is better than no company. isn't it?

When the heavy. arch-shaped door opened Edna Louise looked neither pleasantly nor unpleasantly surprised. She didn't look any way at all except in sort of neutral gear. Her freshly ironed pink dress was tied behind in an abundant bow, and her blond hair fell as always in obedient waves. She looked as though she were going to have tea with the Roosevelts, but Edna Louise always looked like that.

"I didn't know you were coming over," she said in the same tone she would say, "I didn't know the bank closes at four thirty."

While her greeting didn't sound especially hospitable, she did push open the screen door.

Now Edna Louise Jackson is not only the daughter of the richest man in town but she also has the reputation of being a little "boy crazy" so she'll understand why I like Anton.

Over heavy mauve carpeting she led me through the orderly stillness of the living room With its lemony polish anointing the proper mahogany furniture the living room was the saved room in the house. Saved for something sometime when it would be taken out and used.

In the cleanliness-is-next-to-Godliness kitchen, background organ music gave drama to the words of a radio announcer, ". . . The story that asks the question

44

—Can this girl from a mining town in the West find happiness as the wife of a wealthy and titled Englishman?"

I sat down next to her at the kitchen table. "Do you follow *Our Gal Sunday?*" I asked. "It's probably my favorite soap opera."

"I like Sunday and Lord Henry, but I hate Elaine. She tells Lord Henry the most awful lies about Sunday."

"I know."

"Well, why don't they get her out of the story?"

"Because they need Elaine to make the story interesting," I said, surprised that the smartest girl in Miss Hooten's class hadn't figured that out for herself.

"But she's so bad!" protested Edna Louise.

"Without Elaine, Sunday and Lord Henry wouldn't be doing anything but holding hands and strolling through their mansion. What's interesting about that?"

"Nothing," admitted Edna Louise. "Sometimes you have good ideas," she added.

"Oh, well," I said, "I guess I like to notice things like that." With my confidence boosted I decided to tell her about him. "Today I met somebody that I like."

"A boy?"

"Yes. No! He's a man."

"How old is he?"

"Maybe twenty, twenty-one or -two, like that."

"And your mother's going to let you go out with him?"

"Uh, no, I guess not. But he can't go out anyway —he's a German from the prison camp."

"A German prisoner!" repeated Edna Louise. "That's almost as bad as going out with a nigger!"

Repelled by the comparison, I shouted, "It isn't!"

"It is too. God is on America's side and anybody who's against us is on the devil's side, and that's the truth."

"The truth is that he's a very good person," I said with full conviction. "And someday we're going to meet

45

again." Then, hitting upon a way to punish Edna Louise, I added, "And anyway, I have to go home now."

As she adjusted the volume on the radio she called out, "Bye."

5

ON THURSDAY MORNING I boarded the eight forty-five train to Memphis.

At the Skyway, on top of the Hotel Peabody, Grandma and I were seated at a white-clothed table next to the wall of clear glass. As I pointed out the buildings on the bluff, the barges on the Mississippi, Grandma seemed pleased. "I told the maître d' to make certain my granddaughter has the best possible view."

During lunch Grandma spoke of her fears for her two sisters and their families in Hitler-occupied Luxembourg. They hadn't written Grandma, not in months. "Toby's husband, Aaron, is the finest doctor in the country—he treats the Grand Duchess Charlotte." She pressed her handkerchief to her nose. "I know they're all right."

I told her what I had read about mail sometimes being destroyed during wartime. "They're probably worried about you," I said.

Grandma fingered the diamond and platinum bar pin at her neck before looking up cheerfully to ask if I was ready for dessert. When I considered the price of my lunch, one dollar and forty-five cents, I said I was all filled up. But Grandma said, "Nonsense," as she ordered tea for two and persuaded me to try a long chocolate pastry with a French name. And that by itself cost thirty cents!

Later we walked arm-in-arm down busy Main Street, in and out of stores—Goldsmith's, Levy's, and Lowenstein's. Grandma bought me two pairs of shoes and two wool skirts with matching sweaters.

"Next time," she said, "we're going to shop for dress-up clothes."

When she took me to Union Station, I told her it was the best time I'd had all summer and that next Thursday she wouldn't have to spend even a cent on me. "I just want to be with you," I told her.

"Oh. Patricia darling, next Thursday is no good," she said, letting her face show a regret that I mistrusted. "Grandpa and I are leaving the following Friday for Hot Springs."

She went on talking about how sorry she was and that when she returned in August—but I had stopped listening. Why should I care? She's had her children; she doesn't want any more.

"Don't worry about it, Grandmother," I said more shocked by the chill in my voice than the actual words. "It's really not all that important."

I found an unoccupied double seat and stared out the filth-encrusted window until the train began to pull out from the station yard. And not until then did I cry.

The next day I wondered why I had acted so silly, and I wrote Grandma, thanking her for all the nice clothes and "for the beautiful day that we had together."

But outside of that day—that one day—the summer was hot, dry, and endless. Edna Louise. Juanita Henkins. Mary Sue Joiner, and Donna Rhodes had hopped aboard a bus that had taken them away from this flat and fried bit of earth that was Jenkinsville to the Baptist Training Camp up in the Ozarks. During the day they swim, hike, and learn how much Jesus loves them. At night they sit around the campfire roasting marshmallows and singing about how much Jesus loves them.

I asked my mother if I could go if I promised

(cross my heart) not to sing those songs and only to pretend to listen when they talked about Him. "After all," I pleaded, "Jesus isn't contagious." But she said, "No. It's only for Baptists."

So after they went away, the little good in the summer just wasn't there anymore. Ruth was preoccupied with her work and thoughts of Robert, and even Sharon didn't really have time for me. She and Sue Ellen spent practically the whole day, every day, getting in and out of a water-filled galvanized tin tub which was set beneath the chinaberry tree.

There was nobody to talk to and nothing to do. The school library was closed. I had finished reading the books bought with Grandma's ten dollars, and my father made it very clear that he didn't want to catch me hanging around the store.

A few times I rode my bike out to the prison camp. There was always the chance of maybe seeing him. My friend, Anton. Mr. Frederick Anton Reiker. Only thing I ever saw, though, was cattle-wire fencing strung high on Y-shaped poles which squared off a huge, open area. Back a distance towards the center of the treeless compound there were ten or more long whitewashed barracks sitting on their own patches of grass. Not many people were about during the day, although sometimes I did see a prisoner or two walking. But it was never Anton.

Outside of biking, the only other thing I liked doing was fixing up my hide-out. Actually, the hide-out isn't so much a hide-out as it is a forgotten place. It is a perfectly ordinary over-the-garage servants' quarters— one big room, a little kitchen, and bathroom—located halfway between our house and the railroad tracks. But it has been closed up for the ten years that our family has lived in the six-room frame house out front.

There are two important things that make the place secret enough to be called a hide-out. A long time ago my father pulled up the horizontal stair boards to keep hobos from finding a home. I like it that way because no grownup would balance himself on the brace boards to climb up like I do. The second secret point is that the stairs leading up to the hide-out are located inside the garage. so from our house it's impossible to be seen climbing up or down the stairs.

From the hide-out's back window I watched a slow freight rumble noisily down the tracks towards Little Rock. I opened *Webster's Collegiate* to the *F*s. Time to get going on my ambition. It's not the only one I have, but it's the only one I work at. Someday I'm going to know the meaning of every word in the English language.

I let my finger run down the page of the dictionary until it stopped at the first word that wasn't completely familiar: "Fragile." Lots of times boxes of glassware and things come shipped to the store marked: *Fragile! Handle with care*. But it must have more of a meaning than that. I copied the definition into my notebook: "Easily broken or destroyed; frail; delicate." My word of the day.

A few minutes later I climbed down the steps' skeleton and went into the house where I found Ruth leaning over the tub giving Sharon her bath. Up to her belly button in bubbles. it was plain to see that Sharon was in one of her giggly moods.

"Do you know why the little moron—" she interrupted herself with an attack of giggles. Again she began, only to act as though she had been breathing laughing gas.

It was becoming tiresome. "Ruth, you tell me the joke," I said.

Sharon straightened up. "No, let me! Do you know why the little moron took his loaf of bread to the street corner? 'Cause—'cause the little moron wanted to wait to get some jam." Hiccup-like laughter engulfed her and I joined in. Mostly because I had never before heard anybody louse up a moron joke.

I hung around watching while Ruth got Sharon all dolled up in her Shirley Temple dress and Mary Jane shoes for Sue Ellen's sixth birthday party. One thing, and it's not because she's my sister, but Sharon happens to be very pretty. Everybody says that with her black hair and dark eyes she looks just like Mother, while I look like—No, I don't think I look at all like him!

Outside, the two o'clock sun right away showed us that he was far from fragile. "We'll walk slow," said Ruth, "so as not to anger him up."

On the sidewalk in front of the birthday house Ruth adjusted Sharon's pink hair ribbon. "Now don't let me hear no bad reports come back on you, you hear me, girl?"

Sharon nodded, turning to go. "Hold up now!" called Ruth. "Remember what it is you is going to say to Sue Ellen and her mother 'fore taking your leave?"

"I had a very good time at your party and—and ah—" She looked into Ruth's face for the answer.

"And I thank you kindly for inviting me," supplied Ruth.

Sharon smiled. "And I thank you kindly for inviting me," she repeated. And without even a good-bye wave she skipped off into the birthday house.

As Ruth and I walked slowly back, I tried to talk to her, but she wasn't in too much of a mood.

"Ruth—why are you mad at me?"

"Mad at you? Oh, Patty Babe, I ain't mad at nobody about nothing. Sometimes when a person be thinking about one thing it don't mean they is mad about another thing. It don't mean nothing but that they is too busy for normal conversation."

Then it was Robert. Laughing, light-skinned Robert over there fighting in some faraway foxhole. God, would you please remember to keep Robert safe from harm? Please, God, 'cause he's all Ruth has. Amen.

"Want to know who is the strongest man I ever knew in all my whole life. Robert is. I bet he could

51

beat up six Germans and outshoot a dozen of them. Honest he could!"

A slow smile spread across her lips. But her eyes—Ruth's eyes had this gloss and they weren't smiling.

"Oh, Robert's going to be O.K., you'll see. And you know what? Robert's going to help win the war."

"Honey, I don't care about no war. I jest cares about my boy."

"You have to!" I felt embarrassed by the conviction rushing through my voice. "You're supposed to care! Don't you know the Germans will take everything you've got, and then they'll take you into the field and kill you? Don't you know that?"

Ruth laughed. At me? Let her. Let her laugh her fool head off. She's not my mother.

From a deep well between her bosoms Ruth brought out a white handkerchief with printed flowery borders and dabbed at her eyes. "Oh, Honey Babe, I got nothing in this here world worth taking, and no German or nobody else is gonna kill me till the good Lord is willing."

"If you believe that," I said, trying to frame the words, "then why can't you believe it's also true for Robert? No German can kill him unless God wills it."

There was no answer, nothing except the sound of shoes against blacktop. But then her arm dropped across my shoulders, bringing me to her in a sudden hugging motion. "Unless God Himself wills it," I heard her say.

I followed Ruth into the kitchen where a headless hen, its blood already drying on its body feathers, lay on the rubber drainboard. "Sit and talk a spell," she said.

I glanced again at the grotesque bird. "I'll see you when you finish with her," I said, backing away.

Out at curbside even the neat row of houses, mostly bungalows with screened-in side porches, seemed peopleless. Not a soul was about. I pictured the ladies of the houses, sitting with saucerless cups of coffee, their eyes fixed on the kitchen radio as they lived through Mary Noble's trials as a backstage wife, Helen Trent's over-thirty-five search for romance, and poverty-reared Our Gal Sunday's efforts to keep up with the local nobility.

I didn't want to grow up to spend my days like that, but I didn't want to spend my growing-up days like this either. Sitting alone on a curb trying to think of something to do.

If I had a horse as black as the night I'd go galloping off in search of her. Go. Evol, Go! North toward the Ozarks and never come back.

People would ask, "What a peculiar name, and what does it mean?" And I'd lie to them, saying it was short for "evolution." Evolution like in Darwin's theory.

But someday it would happen. I'd find her and she'd understand right away that Evol has more power spelled in reverse. And that would be the sign between us. She would be my real mother and now at last I could go home.

A car passed. Chrome hubcaps mirrored the sun's rays. I began collecting those gray-white stones that were within lazy reach. Improve your aim. Hit the hubcap. Win a prize.

From some distance away, I heard a boy's thin voice calling me. He was short-cutting across our yard, walking as though he wore springs on his feet, up-and-down Freddy Dowd.

The last time I saw Freddy, a week ago, we were playing marbles on the sidewalk and my best agate was at stake. Suddenly he appeared from inside our house, my father. "You get yourself in this house this minute!" As soon as I closed the front door, he was standing there, telling me that he didn't ever want to catch me playing with that Dowd boy, not ever again. I didn't understand why.

"But why can't I? He's very nice."

53

"Are you questioning me?" my father demanded. "Are you contradicting me?"

I told him that I wasn't, and after a while he cooled off and went back to the store. The crisis was over.

But later when I looked outside my bedroom window I saw Freddy was still there waiting for me. So I called down that I couldn't come out anymore, not today, because it was getting close to suppertime; and Freddy nodded before slowly loping away. Later, though, I thought about it, wondering if he could have heard. Feelings are fragile too.

Freddy said, " 'Lo," and sat down next to me. "Hey, whatcha doing?"

"Ohhhh, I'm playing Hit the Hubcap, it's a wonderful game I just invented. I'm having a wonderful time."

"Hey, lemme play."

"O.K., but first you have to gather up the ammunition." I held up a smooth, gray pebble. "Ten for you and ten for me."

Freddy wandered barefoot over assorted road gravel, searching out only the small quality stones he knew I would like. In winter Freddy wore denim overalls with a checkety shirt of faded red flannel, but now he was dressed in his summer attire—the same worn denims without the shirt.

He counted out the stones in a one-for-you and a one-for-me fashion and then sat down on the curb to play the wonderful game. When no car came along, we played Hit the Oilcan.

"Hey! Hey! There's a car a-coming!" shouted Freddy.

I called out last-minute instructions: "Dead center of the hubcap is bull's eye. Hundred points."

Achoo-ey, Achoo-ey. From the sound of its motor it was a tired old thing that used sneezes as a means of power. The car moved slowly into firing range. Then small stones pinged against metal. A single stone revolved around and around the hubcap before firing upward against—crack! *The Window!*

From inside the car a family of faces turned to stare vacantly, like they had all experienced sudden, violent slaps across their faces.

I ran. Oh, God, now what have I done? I ran through our yard, behind our house, and to the field beyond. I ran until my heart warned that it was ready to explode. And then deep in the field I fell down and let the tall grass bury me.

After a while my heart slowed down. Nobody was hurt. It wasn't exactly the crime of the century or anything. Just an accident that I caused, but an accident I could make right. Yes, if only I could find them again. I remembered their car. The sickly sound of it. The lackluster blackness of it. And there, sitting atop the hood, a silver swan with V-spread wings. I could find that car again. At this very minute it was probably parked in front of some Main Street store.

Ruth would loan me the money to pay those folks for a new window, I knew she would. I pictured the scene between the car's owner and me—"I want you to know that it was an accident, and I only hope you can find it in your heart to forgive me." The old farmer would slowly nod his head, taking it all in, before saying that I was a fine, honest girl. Maybe we would even shake hands before saying good-bye.

I got to my feet. Sticking to the front of my damp polo shirt was a layer of field dust and down my knee ran a single rail of dry, red blood. I couldn't remember hurting my knee. As I walked through the field I could hear Ruth singing: "I looked over Jordan and what did I see-e?"

She didn't just sing from her neck up like other folks I know.

"Coming for to car-ry me home. . . ."

Her songs always seemed to come from a deeper, quieter place than that.

I swallowed down the sadness in my throat before going into the kitchen. She sat there at the white metal table shelling a small mountain of peas. Through squinting eyes she gave me a questioning look.

"Honey Babe, you is jest too pitiful-looking for the cat to drag in. You been fighting with Freddy? Now you tell Ruth."

"We didn't fight," I said dully. "I never in my whole life had a fight with Freddy, and that's a terrible thing to say, besides. You sound exactly like my father. Just 'cause Freddy's poor and doesn't dress up you think he's not as good as anybody else. Well, he is, and it says so right in the Constitution of the United States of America: 'All men are created equal.' "

Ruth shook her head. "I asks you if you had a fight and you gives me a history lesson. A person can shore learn a lot of things around here."

I sat down next to her at the kitchen table, but not one more word did she say. It wasn't supposed to happen like that. Gently, even against my will, Ruth was supposed to squeeze the information from me.

I realized it wouldn't happen that way, so I just spilled it out. For a long while Ruth didn't say anything. Then she sighed and asked, "Them folks, did you know them? Was they white folks or colored?"

"I don't remember knowing them, but they were white folks from the country."

Somewhere on her forehead a line deepened, and I knew it wasn't so good that they were white. Ruth pulled down a brown simulated-alligator bag from the top of the refrigerator. "Did those folks know you is Mr. Bergen's girl?"

"No—I don't know. Maybe they did," I said, remembering running towards the rear of our house. Not very smart.

She pushed aside a black eyeglass case and a Bible about the size of an open palm to bring out a red zippered change purse with the printed words, "Souvenir of Detroit, Michigan." Inside the change purse some coins jangled, but all the paper money was pressed neatly into one small square. She opened the three one-dollar bills to their full size. Carefully she refolded them before placing the money in my hand.

"Now you ask the man how much a window costs 'fore you go giving him all your money."

She would do all this for me? There between her neck and shoulders was the warm cove where a head could lie and rest. And there I would be home. Home safe.

Ruth's eyes met mine. Could she know? Could she possibly know? There's nothing to know! I'm not a baby and she's not my mother. I ran out of the back door, letting the screen make a slamming noise.

As I walked toward downtown I noticed a breeze pushing a few elm leaves around without doing much more than promising to cool things off. Still, my thoughts began to tidy themselves up and I felt better. After all, wasn't Ruth on my side? And wasn't I even now going out to right a wrong?

It was then that I saw a green Chevy roaring down the street towards me. My father! For a moment I thought I was going to take off behind one of the houses or maybe hide behind the shoulder-high hedges that separated front yards from public walks. But I didn't. Didn't run. Didn't hide. Didn't anything.

The car passed me and then came backing up to a jerky stop. The door was opened and hurled shut. His face was frozen a bluish whitish color, like all the red blood had iced over. With long strides he came toward me. My back pressed against the hedge.

"Let me tell you what happened. Please!"

It was just noise to him. A mask cannot really hear. He kept coming toward me. I propelled myself backward, falling into and finally through the tight little branches. From across the protecting hedge he commanded, "Come here this instant!" At his temple a vein was pulsating like a neon sign.

"Please give me a chance to explain. It was an accident," I said. "I was aiming at the hubcaps."

He pointed a single quivering finger at me. "If you don't come here this instant I'll give you a beating you're never going to forget."

Did that mean if I came willingly he wouldn't hurt me? His face showed no sign of a thaw. Then I felt the warming spirit of Ruth. "The Lord gonna protect all His children." Fingers crossed, I stepped through the opening in the hedge to stand soldier-straight before my father.

"Closer!"

Only one foot advanced before a hand tore across my face, sending me into total blackness. But then against the blackness came a brilliant explosion of Fourth-of-July stars. Red, yellow, blue, and then green. I never knew those stars were real; I had always thought they were only in comic books. The pain was almost tolerable when a second blow crashed against my cheek, continuing down with deflection force to my shoulder.

Using my arm as a shield, I looked up. I saw the hate that gnarled and snarled his face like a dog gone rabid. He's going to find out someday I can hate too—"Ahhhh!"

Knees came unbuckled. I gave myself to the sidewalk. Between blows I knew I could withstand anything he could give out, but once they came, I knew I couldn't.

Hands that were in the throes of a fit worked to unfasten his belt buckle. Rolling over, I hugged the hedges. He bent low to send the black leather flying.

"Ahhhheeeeehh!" My God! Legs—on fire? After the first flash of piercing pain subsided, my hate roared up strong enough to keep the tears away.

"I'll teach you to throw rocks at people!" he shouted, whipping the belt backwards through space.

"Nooo—ohhhh! Please!" I begged. Can't stand more—can't.

I heard the leather sing as it raced against the air—my eyes clamped closed.

And then they came, ugly and unexpected, those violent little cries that seem to have a life of their own. Short yelps of injury mingled with anger and defeat.

A car door opened and slammed shut. A motor gunned as though for a quick getaway and then roared off.

6

WHEN SATURDAY CAME I was glad. Most country folks stop working about noontime, and by one o'clock Main Street starts jamming up with muddy pickup trucks filled with yellow-haired children.

And there'll be lots of colored folks in town with their kids too, only difference is they'll be all scrubbed and shiny-shoed like it was Sunday. Another thing that's different about them, and I do a lot of listening in on other people's conversations so I know, is how they speak to one another. So respectful and everything. It's as though they try to give each other the respect that the rest of the world holds back.

I mean, if you'll notice how the poor white people talk to one another, mostly they don't even bother to call each other by name. But the colored are different, always remembering to give each other the title of Mr. Somebody or Miz Somebody except, and Ruth told me this, when they go to the same church and then it's Brother Somebody or Sister Somebody.

Saturday has always been my favorite day because my father hires extra salesladies, and he never says a word when I pitch in to help. Working makes me feel useful for a change, and I get to talk with an awful lot of people. If you really, really listen, you can learn things. Sometimes you can learn things people don't even know they're teaching. Like the preacher's wife,

Mrs. Benn, who only last Saturday was talking about the greed of some people, always wanting things. And then in the very next breath complaining how the First Baptist doesn't pay her husband enough so she can buy clothes or hire a Nigra.

From the corner closet, which I share with Sharon, I took out my light-blue middy dress. It happens to be my favorite and not only because I picked it out myself but because it has no sashes, no lace, and it isn't pink. Within twenty strokes of the brush my hair came alive. And it's just the right color hair too—not flashy red or dull brown, but auburn. Alive auburn.

Standing in front of the Victory Cafe, Mr. Blakey was talking to Mr. Jackson. Mr. Henkins pulled his black Oldsmobile into a narrow space, and before he was completely out of the car he called, "Hey, did y'all hear the news?"

"Sure did," said Mr. Blakey. "Heard it on the radio not five minutes ago. Isn't that something? Imagine the FBI catching those eight dirty Nazis 'fore they could do a nickel's worth of damage."

"Know whether they sunk the U-boats?" asked Mr. Jackson. "Sure hope they blew them to smithereens."

"The radio didn't say," said Mr. Henkins. "But they caught all them saboteurs and that's the important thing to remember."

Mr. Jackson became aware of my presence, so I just said, "Hello," while I brushed some imaginary dust from the skirt of my middy before walking into the store. I straightened the story out in a logical sequence so I could tell it in a businesslike way to my father.

He was leaning against the register, taking a long draw from a cigarette.

I walked over. "I came to give you some important news."

"What news?" He blew out smoke along with the question.

61

"The news of the landing in the middle of the night of the German U-boats. Right here on the American coastline." I was encouraged by his head which jutted forward as though he wanted to get closer to the source of information. "Now, the Germans thought they could land saboteurs and nobody would know, but the FBI, through very secret information, found out about the scheme and captured them, all eight of them!"

"Where did you hear that?"

"It's the big news. It was on the radio not five minutes ago." Snapping on the shelf radio, he gave me a look while waiting for the tubes to warm. I tried to figure out just what the glance meant: I'm too young and/or stupid to comprehend a news bulletin; I'm deliberately lying to him; or maybe I'm just having a childhood fantasy.

Finally the radio came on, and right away I recognized the voice of Lorenzo Jones apologizing to his wife, Belle, for buying fishing gear with money from the cookie jar. My father moved the dial—religious music. And again—a commercial for Pepto-Bismol.

"Just wait till the twelve o'clock news," I said, already backing away. "You'll hear about it then."

My mother was busy taking ladies' sandals from their boxes and placing them on a table where a boldly written sign stated: SPECIAL! ONLY $1.98. She worked hard in the store, you have to give her credit for that. And not just in selling or straightening up counters the way the other salesladies do but in thinking up ways "to turn a profit on the new and to get our money out of the old." She was especially good at that because I think she likes the store better than anything else.

Mr. Blakey came into the store, throwing my father a wave. "Harry, didya hear the news? About the Nazi saboteurs? They were planning on dynamiting the Alcoa Plant in Alcoa, Tennessee. FBI caught them with their pants down. Carrying one hundred and fifty thousand bucks in bribe money."

"Yeah, I heard," answered my father. "Patricia told me all about it."

"Patricia told me all about it" echoed in my brain. I had done something nice for my father, and he was pleased with me and he might never again question my honesty. And maybe I had even won the right to work in the store when it wasn't Saturday.

Suddenly I felt greedy; I wanted my mother to be pleased with me too. "Hey, Mother," I said. "Did you hear about the saboteurs the FBI caught?"

She stopped her work to see if I looked decent enough. "Did you and Sharon have lunch?"

I must have passed inspection. "Yes, ma'am."

She went back to unboxing the shoes. "What did y'all eat?"

"Oh, we had some—some—Oh, I know. Leftover meat loaf, and corn on the cob, and some of those store-bought cookies you bought for dessert."

"What're Sharon and Ruth doing?"

"Well, Sharon went to Sue Ellen's, and Ruth is taking all the dishes out of the cabinet. Are we gonna get busy today?"

"No. Why don't you run along—go play with Edna Louise instead of hanging around the store."

Without her even trying, she could get me mad. "Because, like I've told you before, Edna Louise and Juanita Henkins and just about everybody I know have gone off to Baptist Training Camp. And I wasn't planning to hang around; I was planning to wait on customers." I thought of a few other things to tell her too. Things like if she doesn't really want me then I'll go along. She'd be sorry to lose such a good clerk on a busy Saturday. But I didn't say it because I don't think she'd care one bit if I left. Actually, I believe she'd prefer it.

I'll tell her what a good saleslady I am. "Hey, Mother, you want to know something? Last Saturday I sold twenty-five dollars' worth of clothes and stuff to

63

just one customer! Did you know that?" Liar. My best sale was barely eighteen bucks. Damn it, Conscience, go away.

Mother stopped her work to look again at me. Probably she had no idea that I was capable of making such a big sale. "I wonder," she said, more to herself than to me, "if Miz Reeves has time for you today."

Miz Reeves? Miz Reeves from the beauty parlor! "Oh, no! My hair looks fine just the way it is, and I washed it myself only two days ago."

She started walking towards the telephone as though she hadn't heard a word I said. "Let's see if she can take you now."

I ran slightly ahead of her. "Mother, would you please for once in your life listen to me? My hair is the best thing about me. People are always telling me how lucky I am having such naturally wavy hair. And you *know* Mrs. Reeves can't set hair. All she ever does is to make those tight, little-old-lady curlicues."

She picked up the receiver and gave it a crank.

I pressed it down again. "Listen to me! Everybody makes jokes about Mrs. Reeves. They say she only thinks she can set hair because she fixes up the lady customers at the Spencer Funeral Parlor and none of them ever made a complaint. And that's the truth!"

She looked at me, not liking what she saw. "Well," she said, "I'm very sorry you don't think Miz Reeves is good enough for you. You ought to be ashamed of yourself. A girl your age going around looking like you do."

I guess what she really was trying to tell me was that it shouldn't have happened to her. A beautiful woman—everybody says she's beautiful—has an ugly baby girl. Me. A wave of shame flooded over me followed by another wave of full-grown anger. Shame and anger, anger and shame mingled together, taking on something beyond the power of both.

"You listen to me!" My voice was pitched high. "I absolutely will not go and you can't make me. And another thing, if Mrs. Reeves is so good then why do you have to drive all the way to Wynne City to have your hair done? Can you answer me that? And one more thing," I said, looking her straight in the eye, "I don't even like you!"

She pushed my hand away, releasing the hook, and within moments she was smiling her saleslady smile into the mouth of the phone. "Hello, Miz Reeves, how you getting along on such a hot day? . . . Well, you drink yourself a cold glass of iced tea and that'll perk you right up. Miz Reeves, you know who this is, don't you? . . . Yes, that's right. I was just wondering if you could possibly give Patricia a permanent wave right now? . . . Oh, fine. I'll send her over. Bye-bye for now."

A permanent. She did say a permanent. For months and months, a frizzledy freak. Mother walked away, not bothering even to glance at me. From across the store I heard her voice soaring above the other noises. "And you'd think she'd been ashamed of herself going around like that. A girl of her age. And poor Miz Reeves just sitting there waiting for her too."

"Let's just see if she refuses me!" answered my father, coming closer.

Mrs. Fields and her customer, Mayor Crawford's wife, didn't even pretend to be interested in house shoes anymore.

"Har-ry, now don't you hit her!" My good old mother was pleading for me. "She's nervous enough from you as it is."

"Don't you tell me I make her nervous. That's a God damn lie and you know it!"

Mrs. Crawford, what would she think of us? Her pinched little face tilted a bit to the right while her dark owl eyes stared.

Then there he was, standing over me. He just

65

looked down without saying anything. Was he waiting for something? I will not beg or cry—and he won't even be completely certain that I'm afraid.

He looked at his watch. "I'm going to give you exactly two minutes to get yourself over to Miz Reeves's or else you'll get a licking like you never had before in your life. Understand?"

Nod Yes.

"You answer me!"

"Yes, sir."

The most direct route to the door was straight past my father. I wouldn't give him the satisfaction of walking around him. But carefully. There! My arm whispered past his sleeve. When I finally reached the door my breathing came back.

Out on the sidewalk my thoughts jostled and bumped each other fighting to be heard. Break a leg or an arm. Catch a cold or a train. Hide in the hide-out above the garage or under the railroad trestle at the edge of Nigger Bottoms.

Mrs. Reeves's house sat on the corner of Silk Stocking and Main. Its dull brown paint had been flaking and peeling for as long as I could remember. A front screened-in porch sagged toward the center and dusty wooden steps had been waiting a long time for the good, honest feel of a broom. For a while I just stood there, trying to remember the names of men who died fighting for their liberty.

Then, from within the house, a phone rang. My father! I took the three front steps with a single leap, pushed open the screen door, allowing it to slam closed.

"Oh, howdy, Clara," said Mrs. Reeves into the receiver. "How are you a-managing on such a day? The temperature is near about ninety-six degrees, and wouldn't you know it, I'm giving a permanent wave today. . . . The Bergen girl. . . . No, Patty, the oldest one." She laughed a conspirator's laugh into the re-

66

ceiver. "I reckon I can't hardly say you is wrong. Well now, Clara, I'll ring you a little later on. You try and stay cool, you heah?"

She placed the phone back on the hook and turned to greet me. "Ooh-whee, it's too hot for the niggers today. Ain't it awful?"

I sat down in the red plastic chair in front of the washbasin without answering. She droned on, not seeming to notice that I wasn't talking.

Her sharp little fingernails scoured into my scalp. I wondered if her other customers ever objected to those nails, but then I remembered that the kind of customers Mrs. Reeves was used to working on were long past objecting.

"You tender-headed, Patty?"

"No—ma'am."

"You finding much to do with all your friends gone off to camp?"

"Yes, ma'am."

"Miz Henkins told me that Juanita was having the time of her sweet life. Just a-swimming, and horseback riding, and making the prettiest handicrafts that you'd ever want to see."

"Well," I told her. "My father and mother probably might take Sharon and me to Overton Park."

"How come your daddy didn't let you go off to camp with all your friends?" She really wanted to know. Wanted some new little something to spread around about my father. Once I happened to overhear Edna Louise's mother talking about my father—"He's a peculiar man. Even for a Jew he's peculiar."

Mrs. Reeves's lips were sucked together in anticipation of my answer, and I wondered if it were possible that she lived on a diet of persimmons.

"Well, Miz Reeves, I don't know if I should tell you this or not, but—" I wasn't sure myself just where this was going to lead—"somebody told me that they

67

have more mosquiters and black moccasin snakes at that camp than almost any other place in the whole United States of America."

"That so?" she said, impressed as all get-out. "Well, I sure didn't know that—"

I guess she was busy thinking about mosquitoes and snakes because things got quiet. I drifted into myself. Hold me here, old lady, if you must. Imprison me and disfigure me, but my thoughts are all my own.

"You want me to give you a nice cream rinse?" I opened my eyes to stare into her withered face. "It'll give your hair a real nice luster."

"No, thanks."

"I'll call your mother at the store and ask her, it only costs a quarter."

"I don't want it!"

By eleven the heat from the permanent-wave machine was sending steady runs of perspiration down my forehead. And when she finally cut the current at a quarter to one the only dry area on my middy dress was near the hem.

A few minutes later I knew that my hair had come out exactly as I had feared. A hundred frizzledy-fried ringlets obstinately refusing to flow into one another, refusing to do anything but remain separate and individual wire coils of scorched hair.

7

I WATCHED THE late afternoon sun play with rectangles of light against the blue walls of the hide-out. The two rooms and bath had undergone a real clean-up, fix-up. And with the single exception of Ruth's dyeing that worn chenille bedspread a cherry red, I had done it all myself. Not even Ruth could have made the wood floor of the living room or the linoleum in the kitchen and bath any cleaner or shinier.

A couple of times I was close to asking her to come see how I had fixed it up, but I never did. Partly it had to do with the problem of the missing steps. The other part was that I liked to think Ruth didn't know about the secret place. If she did, it wouldn't be so much of a secret anymore.

At the hide-out's back window, the one overlooking our Victory Garden and the railroad tracks beyond, a desk made from two sawhorses and an abandoned board held all my best books. I sat down, letting my hand prop up my head, and feeling the hair that Ruth had taken scissors against when I had come home from Mrs. Reeves. At least the worst of it had been cut away. "Messing up something beautiful," she had said when first seeing me in my frizzled state.

Soon my mother and father would be home and Ruth would be on the back porch calling me in for supper.

Then from outside the window some movement caught my eye. A man with dark hair, denim shirt and pants, running below the railroad embankment. Soon the five twenty to Memphis would be coming down those tracks, stopping at the Jenkinsville station only if there was a passenger wanting to get on or off.

But this man, and even from this distance there was something familiar about him, was running away from the depot. Maybe some poor fellow hoping to jump aboard at that point where the train slows before rounding the curve.

Then it struck me who he looked like. But it couldn't be—he's at the camp. It had to be him! Just like I prayed. God went and sent Anton to me.

The train blew a long whistle. In a single leap I took the steps. I won't lose you, Anton. Not now. I ran through the field faster than I was capable of running.

I could see the black-stenciled *P* on the back of his shirt. I called out, "Anton!" But my voice was canceled by the great engine. Cupping my hands around my mouth, I tried again. "Hey! Anton!"

Still he didn't hear. But just before the train approached, he stopped and hid against the grassy embankment. I ran my labored run, waving my arms like an overburdened windmill.

"Anton!" His head swung around. He looked at me and then up the embankment, and for part of an instant I knew he was about to bolt across those tracks to his death.

"Anton, it's me—it's Patty!"

His face registered shock and then pleasure. An open palm reached out, waiting for me while overhead the train sounded like a thousand snare drums beating in four-quarter time. Our hands touched; I didn't let go till the train passed.

Directly in front of my father Ruth set down the platter of freshly fried chicken along with a skier's

70

mountain of mashed potatoes. On the second trip from the kitchen she carried a basket of hot biscuits and a bowl of mustard greens. I wished that Anton could join the feast, invisible to everyone but me.

My father was saying, "I told him I might not be your biggest account, but I'm not your smallest. Not by a long shot, and when I order six dozen I want seventy-two pairs."

"You should have kept the six dozen you ordered," said my mother. "We're running low on men's dress shoes."

"Don't you tell me what I should've done—not when I can get all the shoes I want at B.J. Walker's."

My mother blotted her lips with a paper napkin. "Oh, sure, you can cut off your nose to spite your face if you want to, but B.J. Walker or any other jobber is going to charge you another fifteen per cent. Then where will your profit be?"

He jumped to his feet, sending the chair to the floor with a crash. "Don't you dare contradict me! Think you're gonna treat me the way your God damn mother treats her husband?"

"Now, Harry, I don't know why you're getting so excited." Her face was a study in martyred innocence.

The insides of my stomach began swirling around. Did I overeat? I looked at my plate. With the exception of a hole that I had excavated in the potatoes, nothing had been touched.

"You know, God damn it. You know! And I hope to hell you croak on it!" His lips were pressed into a thin blue line and his hands were trembling with a rage beyond his ability to control.

"I don't know!" screamed my mother. "And I don't know why you're so mean and miserable."

My head began its circular rotation, matching in r.p.m.'s that of my stomach. Suddenly it came to me—I had a race to win. I reached the toilet bowl in time to

71

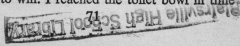

see the mashed potatoes turned green gushing from my mouth, splashing down to the water below.

Since seven thirty I had been listening to the sleep sounds of Sharon. Sometimes I think she's the wisest of us all. She isn't tactless like our mother or nervous like our father and she certainly doesn't always go rushing into trouble like me. I thought about all the trouble I could get into over Anton. My father would beat me, and if other people found out they'd never speak to me again unless it was to call me bad names.

Why did I have to see Anton running to catch that train? Twelve hundred people in this town and it had to be me. Why can't I be more like my sister? Sweet and nice and neat and with enough good sense to stay out of trouble.

Once I figured out that the only thing that Sharon didn't have was enough words. But I could teach her. All kinds. Thin ones like *ego* and *ode*. Fat ones like *harmonic* and *palatable*. And I'd teach her some beautiful ones like *rendezvous* and *dementia praecox*. Maybe (just for variety) throw in some ugly ones like *grief* and *degrade*. And when Sharon knew enough words she could teach me all those things she was born knowing.

At exactly nine thirty the yellow ribbon of light from underneath my parents' door went off. And less than ten minutes later the hard, grating snores of my father carried from the bedroom across the hall.

I put on my house shoes and robe before tiptoeing to the kitchen. He must be starving. In the fridge I found a bowl of leftover chicken that would make the beginnings of a great feast for Anton and me. How about mashed potatoes served cold? I placed everything into one of those brown grocery sacks Ruth is always saving, threw in some biscuits, tomatoes, and apples, and turned the door latch.

"Who's in the kitchen?" my father called out.

"It's nobody, just me."

"Get something and get back to bed."

I unpacked the bag in the darkness and found my way back to my room. Then from a distance a train whistle sounded.

8

I WAITED TILL I heard my father's car accelerate out of the driveway before getting out of bed.

"Well, if it ain't the Sleeping Beauty!" said Ruth. "Morning to you, Miss Beauty."

I yawned a smile and then yawned again as I dropped into my chair at the table.

"How about a nice hot bowl of oatmeal?"

I nodded a Yes and then, thinking of Anton, asked, "Could I please have a couple of hard-boiled eggs too? And leave the shells on."

Spotting the *Memphis Commercial Appeal* on the table, I saw the biggest, blackest headline I'd seen since Pearl Harbor.

FBI SEIZES 8 NAZI SABOTEURS
LANDED BY U-BOATS ON FLA. & N.Y.
COASTS TO BLOW UP WAR PLANTS

Explosives Hidden by Nazis on Fla. Beach
Plan Against Alcoa Plant in Tenn.
Carried $150,000 Bribe Money

Two groups of saboteurs, highly trained by direction of the German High Command at a special school for sabotage near Berlin, were seized by the FBI. The men, all English-speaking, were carrying cases of powerful explosives and $150,000 bribe money.

Under cover of night one submarine released its saboteurs at Amagansett, Long Island.

In possession of the men was a list of special industrial plants they were to sabotage. Sabotage of department stores during their rush hours was also planned, to create panic and to break the morale of the American citizens.

The eight captured saboteurs are thought to be part of a larger underground network already operating within this country. The FBI has rounded up 27 men and 2 women from the New York–New Jersey area. Director J. Edgar Hoover says that many more arrests are imminent.

In Washington, Attorney General Francis Biddle said, "The Nazi invaders will be dealt with swiftly and thoroughly. The Justice Department will try the men for treason."

Articles of War proclaim, "Any person acting as a spy in wartime shall suffer death."

I felt my heart striking against the inner wall of my chest. I'm no spy! I'm not giving information to the Germans. But then again I suppose the Justice Department wouldn't stand up and applaud me for hiding a Nazi? He's not a Nazi! A technicality. A captured German soldier is close enough.

I turned to the inside pages in search of "Li'l Abner" while consoling myself that after darkness came Anton had probably hitched a ride on a freight train.

Opposite the comics there was a smiling soldier from Wynne City with a row of colored ribbons on his chest. He wore his hat at a slight angle to show the world he wasn't afraid.

S/Sgt. Clarence C. "Red" Robbins, son of Mrs. Mary G. Robbins, of 18 School St. in Wynne City, Arkansas, died on June 26 from injuries received at Corregidor.

"It wasn't Antón's fault!"

Ruth brought in a bowl of oatmeal and a glass of milk. "It wasn't whose fault?"

"Nothing. Just something I read in the funnies."

She went back into the kitchen wearing a look of disbelief, and I went back to Red Robbins.

> S/Sgt. Robbins was a member of the 1941 graduating class of Wynne City High School where he was voted "Mr. Personality." He earned his letter playing football.
>
> His commanding officer, Capt. Simpson B. Graves, wrote in a letter to Mrs. Robbins: "Your son was a brave soldier and a splendid patriot."

A brave soldier and a splendid patriot. They were stirring words all right. When you help your country you're a patriot. But if you help the enemy then you're a— Fear pierced the calm of my stomach.

Ruth stood over me, hands on hips. "What you gonna do, girl? Eat it or meditate on it?"

I looked into her face deep below the surface of her eyes where the wisdom is stored. There are answers there all right. Good sturdy answers fashioned by Ruth to fit Ruth. Nothing there in my size.

"I don't know, Ruth," I said. "I just don't know."

By eight thirty the vacuum cleaner was roaring in the living room and the kitchen was all mine. I filled the paper bag with the best pieces of fried chicken, the mashed potatoes, two apples, hard-boiled eggs, and hot coffee tightly sealed in a Mason jar.

Outside the sun was beginning to warm itself for another sizzler of a day, and from the sandbox side of the house shrill sounds of Sharon and Sue Ellen made everything seem like always. I prayed to God that the hide-out would be empty too like always.

Inside the garage I strained my ears for sounds overhead. The creak of a chair? A footstep? But there was nothing. Then I remembered that the very last thing I had heard last night was the whistle of a train. He must have been on that train.

I stuck the sack between my teeth and started the climb up the stair braces. He has to be there. He wouldn't leave without so much as a good-bye. "Anton —it's me. Anton!"

Suddenly the door at the top of the landing swung open and a hand reached down to pull me up and in. "Don't shout my name!" Without touching the shade he bent to look out the window. "Don't you know better than that?"

"I'm sorry. I was afraid you'd gone."

"Well, I'm still here." Anton's frown began to melt into a smile showing a perfect set of white teeth. "And I am happy to see you." He smelled of soap and water, but his face showed the very beginning of a beard.

"I wanted to come back last night," I apologized. "But it wasn't safe. You knew I'd be back, didn't you?"

"Yes, I think so," he said, letting his eyes settle upon me. I turned my head away. I'm not much to look at.

As I ripped open the sack, spreading it flat against the desk like a tablecloth, I felt his eyes still watching me. "I'm sorry about not having a cloth, and I know I should've warmed the potatoes, but—"

"Please!" He lifted an open palm. "It looks good enough to eat." Anton pulled out the desk chair for me. Then, motioning towards the chicken, he asked, "White meat or dark?"

"Oh, no, it's all for you. I'm really not hungry."

Gray eyes flecked with green looked up from the food. "Then we'll wait until you are."

I tried to calculate how long it had been since Anton had eaten. "I'll have something if you want me to."

Anton didn't let a hungry stomach interfere with his hunger for talk. Sometimes maybe a minute or more would pass before a bite of chicken was eaten. And when he spoke his face moved, matching the humor or intensity of his story. He talked about his parents' home three blocks from the University of Göttingen, a home of gables and gazebos where every Sunday afternoon at three, tea was served to professors, students, and long-time family friends.

Anton described his father, University of Göttingen history professor Erikson Karl Reiker, as being "a truly civilized man" for whom the war started back in the early thirties.

The president of the university had summoned him to his office. "Professor Reiker, these unfortunate statements, these jokes, that you are making about the new regime must cease! Did you actually tell your students that Chancellor Hitler sleeps with a Raggedy Ann doll?"

"No, Herr President, I did not. What I actually said was that I *suspect* Chancellor Hitler sleeps with a Raggedy Ann doll."

The president would not be put off. "Listen to me well, my friend. I will not jeopardize this university so that you may demonstrate your wit. If one, just one more of these treasonous remarks comes back to me, then you will give me no choice but to inform the authorities. These are dangerous times and one cannot make such statements and survive."

Anton took a swallow of coffee from the Mason jar. "Late that very night, something—I don't know what—woke me. I followed the light downstairs to my father's study, where I found him sitting, his head resting on his desk.

"He said that he was O.K. and nothing was wrong, but then he began speaking of his grandfather who had once been president of the university. Pointing to the books in mahogany cases that ran the breadth of the room, he said that some of these books were written because Grandfather believed that a president's job was

78

to encourage scholarship. But our current president, he said, would be as comfortable burning libraries as building them."

For moments Anton just stared down at the bony remains of chicken. Then, abruptly, his forehead wrinkled along his hair line as he said, "It wasn't long after that, in the early summer of 1933, when students and S.S. men stormed through the university burning books."

"I wish people would have stood up to Hitler," I said.

"Some people did, but not many. My father chose acquiescence and life rather than resistance and death. Not a very admirable choice, but a very human one."

Anton went silent and I placed a red apple in his hand. "Tell me about your mother," I said. "Do you have sisters and brothers? And, if you don't mind telling me, how did you escape from the prison camp?"

He smiled. "You're a funny one, Patty Bergen. I'll answer your questions—then I'll ask one of my own. Yes?"

I nodded Yes.

Anton leaned back in the canvas lawn chair.

"My mother's minor virtues are limitless," he said as though he was warming up to the subject. "She sings on key, calls flowers by their generic names, and looks like she was born knowing how to pour tea from a silver service. And of her major virtues there are at least two—her warmth and her great sense of fun. She has special ability to find adventure on a trip to the greengrocer. But primarily there is her warmth." He paused to brush away a smile. "I remember once, I must have been all of seven, running home from school, expecting her undivided attention. Instead the house was empty. There was a light on in the kitchen, pots of food simmering on back burners, and I knew she hadn't gone far or for long. And yet there I stood, brimming over with the most inconsolable disappointment."

Anton stopped for a moment, pressed his lips together before confiding, "It's funny, but I might feel something of that today. Now to your question—sisters or brothers? One sister, Hannah, three years younger whom I never had time for." He shook his head. "I'd like another chance."

"You will have one!" I said, totally convinced. "Just as soon as the war is over you can go back to Göttingen, start again. Will you return to medical school?"

"How did you know that?"

"You told me. Remember? The first time we met."

"I'm going to remember that you store information the way squirrels store nuts. Yes?"

"Only if I'm interested," I said. "Well, are you going back?"

"I'm only concerned with now. And from now on I must be free." Anton breathed deeply as though the air outside barbed wire was different somehow.

"But can't you get hurt escaping?" I asked. "And wouldn't you have been free sooner or later anyway? Wars don't last forever."

A crease, like an exclamation mark, sliced Anton's forehead. "What do you know about sooner or later? Is a moment only a moment when you're in pain? For twenty-seven months I've been mostly bored to death and occasionally scared to death." Anton flung his hand out as though giving an emphatic good-bye to all of that. "Well, enough!"

Scared. Anton was a coward! "Our American soldiers aren't scared, do you think?"

"I think it's not in the best masculine tradition to admit it."

"How—I mean, why do you?"

Anton winked. "Because it's just another emotion."

"Sometimes I cry," I said, feeling exceptionally brave admitting it.

80

"And so do I." Anton began laughing as though he was having a good time.

"I'm glad you're here," I said. "I want you to stay safe."

"I will. There's no reason why the Americans should bother with one missing prisoner. An ordinary foot soldier." He adjusted his gold ring, the surface of which had some sort of a crest. "Also, I'm lucky. Twice I've been so close to exploding bombs that only a miracle could have saved me. And so I've had a couple of miracles."

He took a quick look out the hide-out's front and back windows. "But suppose I am recaptured. What will the Americans do? Deposit me in the nearest POW camp where I'll have to wait till the end of the war. But in the meantime this day, this month, this year belongs to me."

Anton began carefully polishing his apple. "What was the last question?"

"I was wondering how you managed to escape?"

"The actual mechanics of the escape are not important," he said. "The pertinent point is that I was able to create a—a kind of climate that permitted the escape. Specifically, my deception was believed because it was built on a foundation of truth. Hitler taught me that."

I heard him say it. "Hitler taught you?"

Anton smiled. "I learned it by analyzing his techniques. Hitler's first layer is an undeniable truth, such as: The German worker is poor. The second layer is divided equally between flattery and truth: The German worker deserves to be prosperous. The third layer is fabrication: The Jews and the Communists have stolen what is rightfully yours."

"Well, I can see how it helped him, but I don't see how it worked for you."

"Because I had a rock-bottom truth of my own," he said, striking his chest with his index finger. "My excellent English. I let it be known that I had had an

English governess. And this gave me the advantage of being considered wealthy. But I didn't have a good workable plan that would capitalize on my believed riches until I saw that pin with the glass diamonds— the one you sold me."

"Yes! I couldn't for the life of me figure out why you wanted it. So gaudy and not at all like something you'd like."

"I loved it!" protested Anton. "Because those glass diamonds were going to make me a free man. One of the guards was a simple fellow with financial problems. One day I told him my father would pay five thousand dollars to the person who could get me out of prison. The guard looked too surprised to answer. But eight days later he followed me into the latrine and asked, 'What's the deal?' 'Five perfect diamonds, each diamond having been appraised in excess of one thousand dollars, will be given to the person who drives me out beyond those gates,' I told him. So he did, and I paid him with a dollar's worth of glass jewelry."

"I'm glad you made it," I said, "but that guard— he could get into an awful lot of trouble."

"I don't feel guilty." His hand rubbed across the slight indentation in his chin. "His concern was for reward; mine was for survival. But, on the other hand, I wouldn't wish to implicate him."

I nodded. "Now I'm ready to answer your question."

His teeth pressed together, giving new strength to the line of his jaw. "I'm certain you appreciate the seriousness of what you have done, aiding an escaped prisoner of war. I was wondering why you were taking these risks on my behalf. Because of your German ancestry? Perhaps your father is secretly sympathetic to the Nazi cause?"

"That's not true! My father's parents came from Russia and my mother's from Luxembourg."

Anton looked alarmed. "I'm sorry. It's just that Bergen is such a good German name."

"It's also a good Jewish name," I said, pleased by the clean symmetry of my response.

His mouth came open. "Jewish?" An index finger pointed toward me. "You're Jewish?"

I thought he knew. I guess I thought everybody knew. Does he think I tricked him? My wonderful Anton was going to change to mean. As I nodded Yes, my breathing came to a halt while my eyes clamped shut.

Suddenly, strong baritone laughter flooded the room. Both eyes popped open and I saw him standing there, shaking his head from side to side.

"It's truly extraordinary," he said. "Who would believe it? 'Jewish girl risks all for German soldier.' Tell me, Patty Bergen—" his voice became soft, but with a trace of hoarseness—"why are you doing this for me?"

It wasn't complicated. Why didn't he know? There was really only one word for it. A simple little word that in itself is reason enough.

"The reason I'm doing this for you," I started off, "is only that I wouldn't want anything bad to happen to you."

Anton turned his face from me and nodded as though he understood. Outside, a blue-gray cloud cruised like a pirate ship between sun and earth, sending the room from sunshine into shadows.

9

ON MAIN STREET, something was different—too many people hanging around for an ordinary weekday better than an hour before noontime. And it wasn't the usual little groups of farmers slow-talking about too many bugs and too little rain. There were quick movements of their hands and high excitement in their voices. "And I'll tell you this—them people would sooner espionage you than look at you."

There were also late-model cars licensed "Arkansas—Land of Opportunity," but with a combination of letters and numbers that marked them as having come from places other than here.

Everywhere this strong current of excitement and pleasure, only slightly disguised, that at long last something pretty big had happened right here in Jenkinsville.

I stood in front of our store, watching the editor of the *Gazette* holding informal court for six of Jenkinsville's leading citizens. Mr. Blakey looked up as a shiny black sedan passed slowly down Main Street. He studied the two business-suited occupants before reporting, "FBI agents from the Little Rock bureau. Those fellers gonna find out this was no ordinary escape. No, sir!"

"Then you figger the POW was fixin' to join up with them eight saboteurs?" asked Mr. Jackson.

"I didn't say that," answered Mr. Blakey. "Still, something's mighty fishy. Harold himself told me that the Nazi was seen sitting on his bunk at five o'clock; at five fifteen he was reported missing; and at five seventeen those Dobermans couldn't find a scent worth picking up."

"What about the train, the five fifteen to Memphis?" asked Mr. Henkins.

Mr. Blakey nodded. "Gone through with a fine tooth. Why, that train was held up for better'n thirty minutes in Ebow." He shook his head. "No, sir, I'm telling you this was no ordinary escape."

Mr. Jackson said, "Quent, why don't you quit saying what it ain't and tell us what you think it is."

Mr. Blakey swallowed down some excess saliva. "If you want my opinion, I will say this—Reiker had to have help. All right, if he had help where did he get it from?" Mr. Blakey was like a champion fighter readying his knockout punch. "Not from inside the camp, I'll wager, 'cause them guards are good clean Americans."

The crescent of men tightened around Blakey. "If you fellers will recall," he continued, "a couple of weeks ago there was this troop train that derailed in California. Before that an Army Air Corps plane up and explodes over New Jersey. And yesterday, the very same day that Reiker escapes, four Nazi saboteurs are landed on the Florida coast while four more land on Long Island. And you want to know what I think? I'm gonna spell it out for you. I sincerely believe that there's a Nazi underground working in this country, and for all anybody knows, it could be working right here among us."

Inside the store I saw that the only activity was over by the hardware. Three farmers were lined up in front of a counter.

My father called for Chester. The black man in his gray porter's jacket came running from the back storeroom. "Yes, sir, Mr. Harry?"

"Chester, go bring up all the twelve-gauge shotgun shells we've got."

"Yes, sir, Mr. Harry."

Two men wearing striped ties and business suits came in the door and headed directly towards my father. I followed them.

"Mr. Bergen?" asked the older of the men as he flipped open a small leather case.

"Yes, sir, I'm Harry Bergen." My father came from behind the counter to shake hands with both men. "What can I do for the FBI today?"

"I'm John Pierce. This is my partner, Phil McFee. We're here investigating the escape of the prisoner from the POW camp." Pierce handed my father a black-and-white glossy photograph. "Do you have any recollections of this man?"

"Once," said my father, "some POWs were brought in here to buy things, but I didn't pay much attention to what those rats looked like."

Pierce pointed to the photograph. "Look carefully, Mr. Bergen. Reiker may have been acting as interpreter for the others."

"Oh, you know, there was one." My father nodded his head up and down. "He was a kinda smart aleck, that one. Tried to joke with me, but I told him right off I wasn't interested in making jokes with Germans."

Pierce struck the picture with his index finger. "Is that the man who tried to joke with you?"

"Well, he might be the one. I'll tell you fellows the truth, I didn't pay much attention to what he looked like. There was one thing I remember. Don't know if it'll help you boys much."

"What?" asked Pierce.

"He talked in a funny way, pretending to be a Harvard boy instead of a convict."

"And there's nothing else?"

"No, sir. I sure wish I could be more helpful to you and Mr. Hoover 'cause he's one of the two greatest living Americans. The other one's General MacArthur."

McFee, who looked as though he hadn't gotten comfortably settled into his twenties yet, allowed his chest to swell to enormous proportions. "Thank you, sir. I appreciate your saying that."

Pierce crossed the store to show the picture to my mother and Gussie Fields, who shook their heads in unison. Then Sister Parker was asked to take a look. She said No and was about to return the photo when she gave a second, more thoughtful appraisal. "You know, he looks a little something like the man Mr. Bergen's girl waited on." Sister Parker turned to find me only a step behind. She held Anton's picture aloft. "Patty, isn't this that German you were talking and laughing with?"

The eyes of the FBI were upon me. I asked, "Is it all right if I look?"

The older agent took the picture from Sister Parker's hand and gave it to me. As a precaution against the shakes, I let my hand rest against the top of the counter. "Well, this might be the same prisoner I waited on. It looks like it could be him only I don't remember his hair being so dark."

"Why didn't you say something before now?" asked McFee. "You've been following us since we entered the store."

"I have a right to be in this store if I want to. It's my father's store."

"You were laughing with him," pressed McFee. "Did he say something funny?"

"No."

McFee's face came in close. "Then why did you laugh?"

"I laughed because—because—" The dam that kept my tears back sprang a leak. "Because he didn't know what to call a pocket pencil sharpener." I hid my eyes in my hands, letting the sobs come at will, regulating their own intensity and volume. Sister Parker put her arm around me, giving me little now, now pats to my shoulder.

My father's voice approached. "What's the matter? What's happened?"

McFee shrugged. "We were merely asking her a few questions and—"

"They made her nervous," interrupted Sister. "Both of them questioning Patty like she went and took that German out of prison."

"Do you realize what you did?" asked my father, grabbing my wrist away from my face. It vibrated wildly like the agitator from some old washing machine. "Look at that child's hand! She's highly nervous and I don't appreciate one bit your upsetting her. I'm going to call the FBI and ask them to give me an explanation for this."

Pierce held his head like he was holding onto a headache. "Now, Mr. Bergen, please—"

"Don't you please me!" said my father. "I want to tell you both something. I'm a Jew and I'd rather help a mad dog escape from the pound than to help a Nazi. Come to my house! Search it from top to bottom, attic, garage, everything!"

"Are you finished talking?" asked Pierce in a voice that just missed being a shout. "Allow me to say this. There is not the slightest suspicion against either you or your daughter. I apologize for my partner who's new with the bureau and sometimes gets carried away. But now that he understands the situation, I'm certain that he'll want to apologize to both you and your daughter. Don't you, McFee?"

"Sure, I'm sorry. I didn't know the girl was a nervous wreck."

"Go wait in the car," barked Pierce. He turned his attention to my father. "I'm going to have to ask you a favor. The escape of the prisoner Reiker may pose a threat to the very security of this nation, and it is considered essential that he be quickly apprehended. We're working night and day to do just that. Now, with that in mind, Mr. Bergen, I'm asking you to please let me talk with your daughter. It's just possible that she might provide some useful thread of information."

I wiped away the last of the tears and said, "I'll tell you anything I can." Just as long as the information is worthless.

Mr. Pierce smiled. "Fine. Fine. As you may have heard, we're fighting the Germans because they're bad, and if one of them gets loose it's very, very important to catch him. The reason we have to catch him is so he can't hurt children and other people. You understand that, don't you?"

"Perfectly."

"That's fine," he said, taking out a yellow pencil scarred by teeth marks. Mr. Pierce jotted down a few words on a stenographic pad as I told my story. He asked me to tell it one more time, adding anything that came to mind. The second time, I remembered the color of the pocket pencil sharpener—it was red.

The agent removed the pencil from between his teeth to inquire whether I had noticed if there was much money in the prisoner's wallet. I didn't remember seeing a lot of money. The agent wanted to know if I was absolutely certain that the only thing the prisoner bought was the sharpener, paper, and pencils.

I thought about the pin with the circle of glass diamonds. "There was something else," I said. "Now that I think of it. The prisoner carried a large tan sack. He must've bought a straw field hat like the rest of the prisoners. Yes! I think he did."

"Would you say," asked Pierce, lowering his voice, "that there was anything peculiar in his behavior?"

"Yes, there was something out of the ordinary about him."

"What was it?"

"Politeness," I said, aware of beginning to enjoy the interview. "He was very polite."

The FBI man muttered a thanks as he walked with weighted steps out of the store.

Across the store, Quentin Blakey and his crescent of men came in to catch the twelve o'clock news: "The FBI has rounded up an additional fifteen spies," said the announcer's voice. "These spies were preparing to help the eight U-boat saboteurs once they established themselves on the mainland. FBI director J. Edgar Hoover said in Washington today that the spies had enough money and weapons to carry out a two-year reign of terror. At two o'clock this afternoon, Director Hoover will give a full report to the President. In Arkansas a prisoner of war escapes," continued the announcer. "That's us!" said Mr. Blakey. "Throughout the country, law enforcement agencies are searching for a German prisoner of war. Frederick Anton Reiker, five feet ten inches, one hundred sixty-five pounds, vanished yesterday from a prison camp near Jenkinsville, Arkansas. The twenty-two-year-old former Nazi soldier is dark-haired, speaks flawless English, and should be considered extremely dangerous. The weather for Little Rock and vicinity is—"

My father clicked off the radio. "Serves them right for coddling those Nazis. Our boys sure don't get that good a treatment when they're taken prisoner."

The president of the Rotary Club nodded. "The trouble with this country is that it's too Christian. The Bible admonishes us to turn the other cheek, but we forget that it also tells us to take a tooth for a tooth, and an eye for an eye."

"I'll tell you something, George," said my father. "I don't think they oughta take prisoners. Not live ones, anyway." There was a chorus of appreciative male laughter.

One of the men suddenly gave George Henkins an alerting poke to the ribs, "Would you looky what's a-coming in the door."

She was young, wearing a tailored dress of sea green, with shoulder-length hair that bounced in rhythm with her walk. But as she came up to the male quartet,

90

they all appeared disappointed. For what looked like dazzling beauty at a distance was at close range only a trim figure and freshly laundered hair.

"Excuse me, gentlemen, I'm Charlene Madlee of the *Commercial Appeal,* and I'm looking for Sheriff Cauldwell. They told me you might know where I could find him."

"I haven't seen Harold since morning," said Mr. Blakey. "You fellows know where he might be?"

The town sign painter, Blister, shook his head. "I reckon with all the 'citement, he's busier'n a hound dog during hunting season."

I followed the lady reporter out to the sidewalk and offered to show her to Sheriff Cauldwell's office. As we drove together down Main toward Front Street I noticed an occasional cluster of men on the sidewalk. Then it struck me. Where were all the womenfolk? Didn't any of the town ladies have bread to buy or an electric bill to pay? It reminded me of a movie I saw: The town men were stationed with guns behind every buckboard, waiting for the Comanches to attack, while all the women and children were holed up in the saloon.

The sun, when did it pull its disappearing act? The complexion of the day had changed to unrelieved grayness.

"There's the jailhouse," I said, pointing to the dirty stucco bungalow with the rippled tin roof that squatted on an open grassy space between Dr. Benson's drugstore and the Rice County National Bank. "The sheriff's office is right inside, but I doubt if he's around today."

She made a skillful entry into something less than a full parking space. "I'll be right back," she said, which I took as an invitation to stick around.

I thought about Anton, alone and getting hungrier. Just as I decided that I'd better hurry back to him with news and food, the reporter returned. "Would you know how to get to the prison camp?"

She followed my directions through the center of

town and then turned right onto Highway 64. "My name is Charlene Madlee," she said, pulling a cigarette from a puffy beige pocketbook. "And I think it's very sweet of you to guide me around."

"Oh, that's O.K.," I said. "I think it must be very interesting being a reporter. How do you become one?"

Charlene smiled. I could tell she liked my question. "What's your name?"

"Patty Bergen."

"Well, Patty, you need to decide whether you have the aptitude—the ability—for it. A good reporter has to have enough curiosity to kill a dozen cats and a love for words. Does that sound like you, Patty?"

"Yes, it does, Miss Madlee, really."

"Call me Charlene."

"O.K., Charlene. Well, I'm very curious and that's one of the things that upsets my father. He says that all I do is ask questions. And I do like words, I use them all the time," I said, stumbling over my enthusiasm. I laughed and so did Charlene. "What I meant to say is that, well, you'll probably think this is strange, but I read dictionaries."

"Really?"

"I keep reading until I find a word I don't know and then I write down the word and its meaning. I got all the way through *Webster's Elementary Dictionary* two years ago and now I'm working my way through *Webster's Collegiate.*"

Charlene turned her eyes from the road to look at me. "How did you become interested in dictionary reading?"

"Well, it's all mixed up with curiosity. When I read a book, I want to understand precisely what it is the writer is saying, not just almost but precisely. And it's the same when people are talking to you. Like a moment ago you used the word 'aptitude,' and because you didn't think I understood, you substituted the word 'ability.' But you didn't actually mean ability. We both know that I don't have the ability to be a reporter today, but I just might have the aptitude."

"That's very well put," said Charlene admiringly. "I'll bet you're a real whiz in school."

"No, I'm not."

"And you're modest too?"

"No, it's the truth. I'm not at all good in school. Mostly I make Cs—sometimes worse."

At McDonald's dairy barn, we left the blacktop to turn right on a dusty side road. Farther in the distance those familiar Y-shaped posts connected a network of barbed wire which squared off the compound. Charlene brought the car to a sudden stop in front of the gate, where two rifle-carrying soldiers marched sentry duty. A third soldier stepped out of a guard house and threw Charlene a salute. "Where are you going, ma'am?"

"I'm Charlene Madlee, a reporter for the *Memphis Commercial Appeal,* and I want to see your warden."

The soldier asked us to wait while he phoned the commandant's office. Within a couple of minutes he returned, shaking his head. "I'm real sorry, ma'am, the commandant cannot see reporters today."

Charlene opened the car door, "You get that commandant back on the phone. I want to speak with him." The soldier's obey reflex had been made strong by constant use. Without hesitation he returned to the telephone. "It's all yours, ma'am," he said, extending the black receiver to Charlene.

"Commandant? This is Charlene Madlee of the *Memphis Commercial Appeal.* Commandant, I have information that suggests that the security of this prison is lax and . . . Of course. Yes, I understand that. . . . No, I know it isn't fair, and that's the reason I drove the forty miles from Memphis just to get your side of the story. . . . First barrack on the left. Thank you."

Charlene shook her head in disbelief. "The commandant just fell for the oldest newspaper trick in the world."

The first barrack on the left was indistinguishable from all the others spread around the compound, with their painted white walls. We came to a stop directly in front of a sign which stated: RESERVED FOR GENERAL STAFF.

A soldier wearing two chevrons on his sleeve approached. "You're the reporter?"

As we followed a few steps behind him, Charlene handed me some sheets of yellow paper and a thick, eraserless pencil. "You really want to be a reporter, then we'll let this be your first assignment. Write down everything that you consider pertinent to the fact that a prisoner has escaped."

The name on the door read: MAJOR ROBERT E. L. WROPER, COMMANDING. I wrote that down. He rose from his desk as we entered. "Yes, happy to see you. Please come right in, Miss Maudlee."

"Madlee," corrected Charlene as she shook his extended hand. She introduced me as her friend, Patty Bergen, "who has the aptitude to become a good reporter."

"Major, what I came here to find out," said Charlene, "is how was it possible for a prisoner to escape this camp?"

He pushed some imaginary strands of hair across a hairless dome. "We're real proud of our security system here, Miss Madlee. We follow the same master plan for security as eighty similar camps across this country —the alarm system, the many security checks, the K-9 Corps of trained Dobermans. Even the exact amount of voltage per square foot of area is written out. And I'm here to see that the orders are carried out according to the master plan." Major Wroper unrolled a blueprint of the camp.

While my writing hand was cramping from the race to get it all down, Charlene seemed to be working at a more leisurely pace. I began to worry that maybe I was doing it all wrong.

Charlene lit her own cigarette with a small gold lighter and blew smoke in the general direction of the officer. "Then, Major Wroper, how is it possible that a prisoner did, in fact, escape?"

"That has not as yet been fully determined. We are not in charge of the investigation, that comes under the jurisdiction of the FBI. But you should know that nothing is 100 per cent foolproof. There's been no prison built that somebody hasn't escaped from."

Major Wroper's statement seemed persuasive. I looked at Charlene to see if she too was impressed. She leaned back in her chair, stretching her legs forward. "But, Major, is it usual to escape without even leaving a clue?"

His eyelids lowered. "Who told you that nonsense?"

"Oh, then there were clues?" Charlene's voice was positively sunny.

"As I've tried to indicate to you, the FBI is in charge of the investigation and—"

"Is it true," interrupted Charlene, "that the dogs were unable to pick up a scent anywhere? Not even from the prisoner's own bed?"

"Young lady, I'd like to cooperate with the press, but I will have to ask you not to write anything that would make us look foolish. I can't have shame brought down on the heads of the loyal men in my command."

Charlene lifted an eyebrow. "Let me assure you, Major, that it is not my intention to bring ridicule upon you or your men. All I want is the information so that I can bring back a story that will make my editor happy."

The officer sighed like a great weariness had overtaken him. "Very well." He picked up an index card and read, "The escapee's name is Frederick Anton Reiker. Serial number GL 1877. Rank: Private, German Army. Height: 5 ft. 10½ inches. Weight: 165 pounds. Age: 22. Born: Göttingen, Germany. Prison

Record: Co-operative. Health: In May Reiker was hospitalized in the prison infirmary for appendicitis." He pitched the card across his desk. "At exactly four fifty yesterday afternoon the prisoners of Barrack 314, having eaten their evening meal, filed out of mess hall. A few minutes later Reiker was sitting on his bunk with another prisoner named Blinkoff. Reiker was reading his palm. At five seventeen roll call Reiker was reported missing.

"A general alarm was sounded and the camp dogs were immediately taken to Reiker's bunk, but they were unable to get his scent. This was due without doubt to the fact that Reiker had had three other prisoners sitting on his bed for palm readings. The dogs were hopelessly confused. A search was made for Reiker's clothing and personal effects, but nothing was located."

Major Wroper rotated his swivel chair toward the window. His eyes seemed to scan the grounds for the prisoner who, like a pair of reading glasses, would turn out to be only temporarily misplaced.

It was Charlene who broke the spell. "Major, did Frederick Reiker escape prison to join forces with the eight saboteurs?"

"I have no reason to believe that."

"What I would like to do now, with your permission, is to speak with some of the people who knew Reiker."

"Oh. Yes, indeed," he said, pressing a button. The door opened and the corporal appeared as quickly as a genie. Major Wroper explained Charlene's request and told the soldier to offer, "all assistance."

We followed the corporal into the outer office where he began making phone calls. A clock gave the time at five minutes till two. If only I could get some word to Anton. Let him know. He must be hungry and worried.

The corporal hit the receiver back onto the hook.

"I'm sorry. It looks like everybody's out on work detail."

"Then take me over to your infirmary," said Charlene.

Inside the infirmary, the smell was all soap and Lysol. The corporal led us past a ward with two dozen white-sheeted beds, but only five or six patients. At the end of the hall he opened the door where a sign read: CAPT. GERALD S. ROBINSON.

A crew-cut soldier with a single chevron sat in a cluttered outer office two-finger typing. Captain Robinson, a small fastidious man, stood up behind a large untidy desk when we entered. "Interesting," he said, giving Charlene a smile. "The FBI hasn't yet been around to interview me and I may have known Anton Reiker as well as any American in this camp."

"Lucky I found you, Doctor, or should I call you by your military title?"

"Oh, you probably should, but don't."

"Dr. Robinson, would you say that the escapee was a tough kind of a prisoner?"

He selected a pipe with a curved stem from a rack of six. "I'd say so, but not in the conventional sense. It seems to me that Reiker has a toughness of mind. In medicine when a person is in constant contact with a disease and yet is able to resist catching it himself, then he would be considered to have great resiliency or, in street parlance, toughness." The doctor looked at Charlene. "Do you know what I'm talking about?"

"Yes!" I said with a suddenness that surprised me. "His mind was strong and clear, and he didn't believe what the Nazis wanted him to believe!"

"More or less," said the doctor.

"Then in your opinion," said Charlene, "he didn't escape for the purpose of joining forces with the eight U-boat saboteurs?"

"Oh, I suspect he wanted his freedom and nothing more."

97

"But, Dr. Robinson, isn't it a distinct possibility that Reiker was merely faking an attitude that he could later use to advantage?"

He took a long puff from his pipe. "It is possible, but I doubt it. Some of our prisoners, mostly former members of the S.S., are truly fanatical men. They're arrogant and they don't care who knows it. Reiker wasn't cut from that mold. He was a scholar, interested in books and ideas. And, perhaps more important, he was a loner."

"This is very interesting, but could you give me a concrete example of something that the prisoner said or did that gives you this impression?"

Dr. Robinson leaned deep into his chair. "I can't honestly remember specifically anything that he said, only—"

Charlene's body pitched forward. "Only what?"

"It was only that he seemed like a decent man."

Before the prison gate stood the same obedient sentry. His eyes swept over the blue sedan before calling, "Proceed, ma'am," as Charlene blasted off, leaving behind a trail of raised dust.

Charlene didn't say anything, and I was grateful for the chance to remember the doctor's words. It was then that I experienced the last of my fear taking flight. Nestling down in its place came exultation. At this moment on a dusty back road within smelling distance of McDonald's dairy barn I felt the greatest joy I had ever known.

10

CHARLENE IDLED THE MOTOR in front of the store. "Nice having you with me today. Would you like me to send you an autographed copy of the story?"

"Yes, thanks very much."

"And if I can ever help you in any way—"

"Well, maybe I could write you a letter?" Why would she want to hear from me? "You wouldn't have to answer, well, I mean, unless you have the time."

"Tell you what, next time you're planning a visit to your grandparents, write me. I'll show you around the paper; it should be very interesting for a girl who has the aptitude to become a reporter."

A reporter? Was it true that just a couple of hours ago I thought about becoming a reporter? Then the word journalist had had a ring to it, but now it's gone. A journalist's life might be fun but fun, like champagne bubbles, can't completely fill you up. Anyway there was something else I'd rather do with my life.

I wanted to run the two blocks home but I remembered Anton's advice to do what I've always done and to go where I've always gone. "Be visible," he had said, "highly visible." I walked visibly into the store. He might like a couple of Hershey bars for dessert.

My father's voice caught me. "What are you doing wandering around? I want you to go right home and stay there. There's a criminal loose!"

"Yes, sir, I know. It is all right if I fool around the yard?"

"Well, stay in the yard where Ruth can keep an eye on you. And, under no circumstances, go farther than the garage."

"Oh no, sir, no farther."

The tub water was only lukewarm against my foot as it gushed from the "hot" faucet, and after a minute it became uncomfortably cool. As I dried myself I wondered if I would ever trade this body of sharp, thin lines for something more gentle, more womanly. "Ruth," I called out from the bathroom, "do you have something for me to eat? I'm starved!"

"Since when you begin asking for food? And taking baths without being told?"

"Since always," I said, buttoning up a fresh white shirt.

Ruth shook her head. "When God went and parted the Red Sea for the Israelites that was a miracle too."

The brown paper bag felt heavy between my teeth as I climbed up the stair ribs. A scent of salami liberally seasoned with pepper and garlic assaulted my nose and started up a series of small sneezes. As I sneezed only an arm's length from the door, I became frightened that he would be frightened. But before I could call his name, his hand reached down and touched mine.

"*Gesundheit!*" he said, and smiled as though I was somebody special.

"I brought you lunch and some fresh clothes," I said, surprised at my matter-of-fact tone.

As Anton measured the Palm Beach trousers against his waist I reached back into the sack and touched cardboard. The box was cocoa-brown, and the cover came embossed with three golden acorns, the symbol of Oak Hall, the finest men's store in all of Memphis. Inside was the shirt, the Father's Day present. Not the Father's Day of a few weeks ago, but of a year before that.

I remember how important it had seemed then to give something special, something of value. At first my mother and I went to Goldsmith's, Memphis' largest store, and we found this perfectly nice sport shirt that she tried to talk me into buying. "And you'll have two whole dollars left over from your birthday money to buy something nice for yourself," she told me. When I said I wanted to walk over to Oak Hall to see their shirts, she got all worked up. "It's just plain stupid to pay two dollars more for a label. You got so much money you can throw it away? Don't you know labels are worn inside the collar where nobody can see them?"

But because my determination outdetermined her determination, she told me to go by myself. I was to meet her back in Goldsmith's in exactly one hour on the fourth floor, better dresses. One whole hour of my very own. Freedom, freedom. I felt happy and practically grown-up. So I took the scenic side trip up in the elevator to the seventh floor book department.

Over a table, a sign decorated with a painted Teddy bear said CHILDREN'S BOOKS. Some were books that I had long ago passed through. *A Treasury of Mother Goose* and Beatrix Potter's *The Tale of Peter Rabbit*. Then there were the Bobbsey Twins and *Winnie-the-Pooh*. On the next table were stacks of the Hardy Boys and good old Nancy Drew. Her father is a hot-shot lawyer, but it takes Nancy to solve all the mysteries.

It was in the adult section that I found the books I wanted to take home. *The Best Stories of Guy de Maupassant* and another collection by O. Henry. Goldsmith's had some good books, beautiful books, and five dollars would buy two or three.

When I glanced up I saw a saleslady starting towards me, and I knew if she just said, "May I help you?" I'd buy de Maupassant and O. Henry. But instead I turned and half-walking, half-running made it back into the elevator with integrity and five dollars still intact.

Inconspicuously printed on the store window in gold Gothic letters were the words, OAK HALL SINCE 1887 and just underneath, three golden acorns. Inside the heavy brass door a middle-aged manikin posed majestically with riding stick. He wore a deep-blue shirt. with a Paisley ascot at his neck.

A carefully attired salesman who, like the acorns, must have been with Oak Hall since 1887, took out stacks of size fifteen sport shirts from behind a sliding glass door. Many of the shirts were marked five and six dollars and some cost as much as ten dollars. One was the exact shirt worn by the manikin. The buttons were pearl, but dyed in perfect matching blue. My hand glided across the fabric, which had the smoothness of marble. The label read, FINE EGYPTIAN COTTON. It was a shirt for presidents and premiers, princes and polo players.

It took only a few minutes' wait for the initials "H.B." to be ironed onto the pocket. But it was only by the greatest amount of self-control that I was able to check my impulse to present the shirt to my father that very night. Actually I did cheat, but only a little, when I told him that I had bought him a perfectly wonderful Father's Day gift.

When Sunday finally arrived I felt the way I used to feel about Christmas. My imagination had played the scene over so many times. I knew that he would be pleased with my gift. He'd say it was the finest shirt he'd ever owned. And then the focus would shift from gift to giver and I would rest there in his arms like a long-lost daughter come home.

The reality wasn't like that. He opened the box, said "Thanks," and then, replacing the cover, he tossed it casually out of sight. But it's what happened next—what I did next—that even now makes me feel the painful pinch of shame. I brought the shirt back to him. "Look, it has your initials, H.B.," I said. "And see the buttons, genuine pearl dyed to perfectly match the fabric which is very special too. Comes all the way from Egypt."

With a sudden half swing of his hand, he pushed both me and the shirt out of his way. "I *said*, 'Thank you,'" he said, edging each word with finely controlled irritation.

Anton asked me to excuse him while he went into the bathroom to change into the pants. It was then that I handed him the cocoa-colored box. "A shirt. You'll need a shirt." I turned my head away. Maybe it isn't such a great shirt. Maybe he won't like it either. But I turned my head back just in time to see his face change from surprise to pleasure. His hand stroked the blueness and his fingers even stopped momentarily to examine a button.

"Thanks," he said, touching my cheek with his hand.

Then he was gone and the room seemed emptier than it had ever before been. Probably it was just that before Anton the room had grown accustomed to its loneliness.

Anton came back, filling it up. His eyes looked blue now, very blue, like the shirt he wore. During our lunch I told him about all the excitement in town, and about my visit to the prison camp. He seemed confused by it all, especially about my interrogation by the FBI.

"Why is there such interest in me? An ordinary soldier."

"Only because they think you're a threat to our national security."

"Me?"

"Because of the German saboteurs from the U-boats the FBI captured. They think you escaped to join up with them."

"U-boats were here, Patty?"

"They just stopped long enough to let off the saboteurs."

"And they think I—"

"Yes."

"It was the timing. It was the worst possible timing!"

"But you're safe here, Anton. You can stay here till the end of the war! Nobody knows about this place and I can bring you food and books to read and anything else that you want—tell me what you want!"

Anton raised his eyes to look at me without raising his head. "A bit of your courage, P.B."

"P.B." he called me, and my initials took on a strength and beauty that never before was there. And now that I had of my own free will broken faith with my father and my country, I felt like a good and worthy person.

Anton laughed, keeping it well within his throat. "After the war when I'm with my family again I'll tell them about you. How an American Jewess protected me."

I searched through his words for even a slight implication that when he was with his family again I'd be there too. But I couldn't find it. I was close to coming right out with it—asking him, begging if that would help, to let me go where he goes.

Then my hand brushed across my hair and I felt the forgotten—the tizzledly, frizzledy handiwork of Mrs. Reeves. The moment went sour.

"Tell me," he said, showing a perfect set of teeth like an advertisement for toothpaste. "Why have you suddenly taken the vows of silence?"

A knot of anger rose up. Anger towards Mrs.

Reeves who uglified me, towards Anton who pretended not to notice, but mostly against myself for believing that a prince could love a plowgirl.

"If I talked less would you talk more?" he asked, still showing off his teeth. Show-off!

"No! It's only because—because I don't feel like any more talking. You want coffee? I'll bring you coffee." As I reached for the door, I saw his hand reach out towards me. But I closed the door firmly between us.

I found myself in front of the house and sat down on the steps, out of view of the garage. The carousel inside my brain began its revolutions: He's nice to me only because I'm useful. He's nice to me only because he likes me. He's handsome. I'm homely. Love is blind and beauty, skin deep. He's laughing at me—with me. With me. Why did I have to find him? How could I endure losing him?

My head dropped forward and rested in the dark hollow of my hands. Remember what they say? My father, mother, the clerks in the store, and the salesmen with heavy sample cases from Memphis, St. Louis, and Little Rock: "You only get what you pay for."

From somewhere a voice called my name. My eyes remained closed. At any moment he'll sit down next to me, and after a little quietness he will ask me to go away with him. "You really want me to go with you?" He'll nod his head, and I'll say, "Yes, Anton, yes."

"Looky here!" said the voice close up. "I got me some salt pork for crawdading."

Freddy Dowd! "I don't want to catch any crawdads, Freddy. I might have a headache." How do you tell a boy who never has anything more to brag about than a piece of salt pork that you want him to go away? Poor Freddy, so thin, like he never quite gets enough to eat.

He sat down next to me. "Salt pork is what them crawdads would rather eat than anything in this here world."

"Have you ever tasted crawdad, Freddy?"

He laughed, showing jagged areas where his teeth had darkened and decayed. "Crawdads ain't for eatin', they'se for catchin'.'"

"Did you know that crawdads are in the same family as lobsters and crabs? The crustacean family, and only people who are very, very rich can ever afford to taste them."

He looked at me like I was telling him the stars are stuck to the heavens with little bits of cellophane tape. "I'm a-gonna ask my daddy," he said after an interval.

Freddy is getting very close to being twelve years old, and he still believes that being a grown-up man is the same as knowing things. Daddy Dowd is a big, slow-moving, slow-speaking man who delivers milk, but drinks something else. Poor Freddy, you're not going to find many answers there.

O.K., so Freddy is simple. There are worse things than that. There's hypocrisy, for example, pretending to like somebody just so they can keep you safe from the FBI. And with Freddy a person can feel comfortable because from his miserable perch he's not likely to be laughing at anybody. Sometimes I feel Freddy and I are related. Well, not exactly related as much as we share something that makes us both outcasts.

Part of our outcastness has to do with simple geography. He is a country boy who because of some accident of his daddy's job lives right here in town. And my geography problem is in being a Jewish girl where it's a really peculiar thing to be. Even when I went to Jewish Sunday school in Memphis the geography thing was still there. I would come in on a cold Sunday morning wearing short-sleeved, short-legged

106

union suits under my sash-tied dresses, while the other girls looked as though they were born into this world wearing matching sweater and skirt outfits.

It struck me that neither of us had said anything for a while. I looked over at Freddy who was busily picking at a piece of scab. How like Freddy to sit quiet and amuse himself when I don't feel like talking. One thing you can say about him is that he's appreciative. He's just happy having someone to sit with.

Leaving downtown was the familiar roar of a car motor. (Did all Chevys sound angry?) It must be six o'clock. Moments later I watched my father steer a wide turn in front of the house and gun the car up the gravel driveway.

"Oh, Harry, leave her alone!" cried my mother through the open car window.

Me? What did I—oh, God, it's Freddy! Where do I keep my mind?

"Go, Freddy!" I whispered. "Go home!"

The car door slammed shut. My father's face was a pasty white. "How dare you disobey me!"

"Please let me explain something to you." My hands automatically reached out in a gesture that looked futile even to me.

My mother stationed herself between us. "Now, Harry. Harry, leave her alone. Please!" With one hand, he gave her a strong push that sent her staggering backward across the grass.

"God damn you!" he shouted at me. "You'll obey me if it kills you!"

My legs were carrying me in reverse toward the rear of the house. "Let me at least tell you what happened. I was sitting there and he just came over a moment ago and sat down. I swear to God that's the truth!"

His feet came faster and I moved to keep space between us. The sounds of Ruth's kitchen radio tuned into the gospel station poured out the open window. "Op-pressed so hard they could not stand. Let my people go . . ."

We were deep into back-yard territory and my eye caught sight of the garage hide-out. God! Don't let him see this. I tried to maneuver back toward the front of the house, but my arm was caught with an explosion of pain.

"Awllll!" My arm felt as if it was pulled out of its socket. Then the barrage. "Noooo-ohhh." The ground reached up and laid me down. Oh, God, can't you help?

Everything was quiet. Was it all over? It seemed too quick to satisfy him. I forced my eyes open. He was standing over me, the brown of his suit in perfect outline against the white of the garage. His breath was coming in quick, heavy gasps and I began to hope that his exhaustion would cut short the agony.

Metal clicked against metal. A leather belt rushed through fabric loops. As the belt whipped backward, I saw Anton with raised fists racing toward my father's unsuspecting back.

"Nooo!" I shouted. "Go way! Go way!"

The belt came down. "Ohhhh-nonono!"

Anton, his hands outstretched before him, froze. His face was like I had never seen it, dazed with horror. Then he clapped his hands to his eyes and backed towards the garage.

11

"SHE HAS TO BE taking it home with her; I can't think of any other explanation. That kosher salami cost one dollar and ten cents." My mother repeated the price a second time for added emphasis.

I pulled the top sheet over my head to block out the early morning sounds from the kitchen and rolled over a now very warm ice bag and remembered. In another few minutes they would be leaving for the store. Only then would I get out of bed. Just as soon as my mother downs her second cup of coffee and my father finishes his corn flakes. As long as I can remember it has been corn flakes and nothing but corn flakes. He's got the same loyalty towards cars. "I'll buy any kinda car as long as it's a Chevrolet." And cigarettes too. He's never had a cigarette in his mouth that wasn't a Lucky Strike.

"So you'd better talk to her, Harry."

"Talk to who?"

"To Ruth!" Her voice hit a shrill note. "I want to know what's happening to the salami and chicken and all the other food that's been disappearing around here lately."

"Well, how do you know she's taking it home? I don't know what you're talking about. But she'll be coming any minute now, and if you want to fire her it's fine with me. Something about that woman I never liked."

I didn't want to speak to them, but I didn't want them to suspect either. I yelled out, "I'm sorry about the salami 'cause I ate most of it myself. And about the leftover chicken, Sharon and Sue Ellen ate the last of it."

"Now you see that!" he told her. "Don't ever talk to me again about missing food."

I'll have to say this for him, he's always generous about food, even when we eat in restaurants. Like that Sunday in Memphis not too long ago when we ate at Britlings' and I ordered the chopped sirloin steak and he said, "That's nothing but a hamburger. Wouldn't you like to have a real steak?" My mother didn't like the idea of ordering "an expensive steak that will just go to waste." But my father told her to mind her own business, and that as long as he lived I could eat anything I wanted.

The phrase, "as long as he lived" sounded like a vague prophecy, and I became sorrowful that he might die now that he was being good to me. I became so sorrowful, in fact, that it was Mother's prediction that was soon fulfilled. An expensive steak went to waste.

The familiar sounds of a spiritual—Ruth was passing below my window on her way to the back door. "Morning, folks," she called. "Well, I heard the weatherman say we're gonna get us a little rain by afternoon, enough to cool things off." My mother agreed that a little shower would be very nice. "Is that piece of toast all you've had to eat?" asked Ruth. "That's no kinda breakfast, Miz Bergen. I could make you some hurry-up griddle cakes."

"Griddle cakes are fattening. Besides I have to leave now."

A couple of minutes later the car backed out of the garage, the motor gunned for the two-block trip, and they were gone.

110

Ruth came into my room, bent over and picked up the flowery chenille bedspread that had fallen to the floor, and asked, "Are you feeling all right?"

I remembered who had brought me the ice bag and aspirins for my head and the ointment for my legs. "I don't know. I guess I am."

From the other twin bed came a long, low, early morning sound as Sharon flopped over to a better dreaming position.

"Come on into the kitchen," whispered Ruth as she tip-toed out of the room.

The marshmallow slowly began to bleed its whiteness over the steaming cup of chocolate. On the shelf of the breakfast room's built-in cabinet our one surviving goldfish, Goldilocks, began her vigorous after-breakfast swim.

"How come that fish got sense enough to eat her breakfast and you don't?" asked Ruth as she sat down at the table.

I ignored the buttered toast and scrambled egg, but took a long drink of the now lukewarm chocolate. "Don't know except maybe Goldilocks has a better cook than I do."

"Must be the truth," Ruth smiled, showing her left-of-center, solid-gold tooth. "You know what you needs, Honey? One of them fancy Frenchmen who cooks up a fine dinner and jest 'fore serving it, he sets it all afire."

We sat for a while in silence, Ruth taking small now-and-then sips of coffee while I sat stirring my chocolate and watching Goldilocks. Ruth's spoon made an attention getting noise and I saw that those brown eyes were upon me.

"I want you to tell Ruth the truth about something. You hear me talking, girl?" I nodded Yes.

"You tell me who is the man."

"Man?"

"Honey Babe, you can tell Ruth. The man that ran out from the garage. The man that wanted to save you from your daddy."

"That man—the man—the—" My voice was still in some kind of working order even if my brain did just up and die.

How can those eyes that rest so lightly see so deeply? And from them there is nothing in this world to fear. "The man is my friend," I said at last.

"You got him hid up in them rooms over the garage?"

"Yes."

Ruth sighed like she sometimes does before tackling a really big job. "He's not the one the law's after? Not the one from the prison camp?"

"Yes."

Her forehead crinkled up like a washboard. "You telling me, Yes, he's not the one?"

"No, Ruth, I'm telling you Yes. Yes, he's the one."

Ruth's head moved back and forth in a No direction. "Oh, Lord, why are you sending us more, Lord? Don't this child and me have burden enough?"

I stood up and felt this sensation of lightness, near weightlessness, like somebody had just bent down, picked up, and carried away all my trouble. My arm fell across Ruth's shoulder. "Everything'll be all right, honest it will." Beneath my arm, there was no movement, no feeling of life. I squeezed Ruth's shoulder and a hearable breath rushed through her nostrils. "You know how you're all the time helping me because you're my friend? Well, Anton's my friend and I have to help him, you know? Don't you know?"

"I don't know what it is I know," she said in a weighted voice.

In the pantry there was plenty of peanut butter,

112

but the jar of strawberry jam was only fingernail high. I turned on the gas burner under the aluminum percolator. I began to worry that maybe prison camp food was better than this, but at least the loaf of white bread was yesterday fresh.

Ruth followed me into the kitchen. "Honey, them peanut butter and jelly sandwiches ain't no kinda breakfast for no kinda man." She looked up at the kitchen clock. "After I bring Sharon down to Sue Ellen's I'll fix up some hot griddle cakes with maple syrup and a fresh pot of coffee."

I threw my arms as far around Ruth's waist as they would go and tried to lift her up by the pure strength of my will.

"Oh, Ruth, you're good, good, good!"

"Now, girl, don't go 'specting no amount of praise to turn my mind about 'cause my mind ain't come to no clear thought yet. All I knows for sure is that I'm gonna fix up a proper breakfast for you and the man."

"O.K., thanks, but would you mind not calling him the man, 'cause he's my friend, Anton. Mr. Frederick Anton Reiker. You may not know this, but you and Anton are all the friends I've got."

Ruth nodded slowly. "I understands that, Honey."

That understanding made me want to tell her everything all at once. "Ruth, he talks to me and he tells me things because I'm his friend. Ruth, he likes me. He really and truly likes me."

"I knows that too."

My heart swelled up for if Ruth knows it, it must be the truth. "How do you know that? Tell me how you know!"

She gave my arm a couple of short pats before finding my eyes. "That man come a-rushing out from the safety of his hiding 'cause he couldn't stand your pain and anguish no better'n me. That man listens to the love in his heart. Like the Bible tells us, when a man will lay down his life for a friend, well, then there ain't no greater love in this here world than that."

Before I reached the landing I heard his footsteps, and then the door opened. I felt certain he was smiling a welcome, although I was looking past him into the familiar interior of the room much as I would look past the brilliance of the sun.

"How are you?" he asked, making it sound more like an inquiry than a greeting.

"Fine." Cowardliness kept me from looking at him. "Did you sleep O.K.? Were you too hot?" I asked.

"No."

The shortness of his answer frightened me. Maybe it's disgust for what he saw yesterday. My eyes shut in a feeble try at pushing away the memories.

"Sure you're all right?" His eyes were on the red raw stripes that crisscrossed my legs.

I moved quickly to the opposite side of the desk. "Oh, yes, thanks."

"About yesterday—"

"It's O.K."

"No," he said with a force I had never heard him use before. "It's not O.K.! Listen to me, P.B. What happened yesterday bothers me. Tell me if I was in any way responsible." Between his eyebrows there was a deep crease, a mark of concern—for me.

All that painful dabbing of layer after layer of face powder that I subjected my legs to may have been a mistake. Concern might be a little like love.

"It wasn't you," I said. "You weren't responsible."

"Then what? Please tell me what you did to deserve such a beating?"

How could I say in words what I couldn't really understand myself? Sometimes I think it's because I'm bad that my father wants to do the right thing by beating it out of me. And at other times I think he's beating out from my body all his own bad. My head began its confused revolutions.

"Come over to the window," I said finally, pointing toward the tracks. "See over there? The shack with the tin roof? There's a boy who lives there who my father told me I'm not to have anything to do with. Yesterday he saw Freddy sitting next to me on our front steps." I told Anton about sleepy Freddy who cuts grass in his spare time so he can make enough money to sleep during the Saturday matinee. Scholarly Freddy who has been in Miss Bailey's fourth grade for two years because he's finally found, "The one teacher I likes." Fearless Freddy, brave hunter of crawdads. And generous Freddy who once bought me the gift of not quite half of a melted mess of a Hershey bar.

"He sounds perfectly delightful," said Anton with a smile. "But why is your father so opposed to him?"

"Maybe it's because he's so poor, but I'm not sure."

He looked a little perplexed. "Why don't you inquire?"

"I can't inquire." My words had a harshness that I didn't intend. "In my father's vocabulary to ask why is to contradict him."

"I don't like him!" The words seemed to dash out. Then Anton caught my eyes as though asking permission.

"Oh, that's O.K.," I said pleased that Anton was taking my side. "I'll tell you something I've never told anyone before. If he weren't my father, I wouldn't even like him."

"But because he is, you do?"

"Oh, well, I guess I—" Then the image came. The image of his thin, rabid face. "I guess I don't too much. No, I don't like him." That was the first time I had even thought anything like that myself. Funny, but Edna Louise once told me, "Your daddy is so sweet." Probably because every time he sees her he says, "Edna

115

Louise, you sure do look pretty today." To Edna Louise he has to say nice things as if she weren't conceited enough.

"Do you have any idea where your father went—what he did immediately following the beating he gave you?"

"Not exactly, I could guess. He probably went into the house, smoked a Lucky Strike cigarette, washed his hands, and ate a perfectly enormous supper while he listened to the evening news."

"Not true. He stood watching the housekeeper help you into the house. Then he came into the garage and talked to himself. Over and over he kept repeating, 'Nobody loves me. In my whole life nobody has ever loved me.' "

"Anton, it must have been somebody else. That doesn't sound like my father."

"It *was* your father."

"I don't understand. Why? How could he be so mean and then worry that he isn't loved? It doesn't make sense."

Anton shook his head. "I met your father once; I interpreted for some of the prisoners who came into the store."

"I remember! You said the prisoners needed hats to protect themselves from our formidable Arkansas sun."

Anton smiled, and the smile made him look very young, more like a boy my age than a man. "How could you possibly remember that?"

"Easy. Nobody from around here says things like that. I also remember that he didn't think your remark was very amusing."

"I can believe that because—" Anton paused like he was trying to put some new thoughts into good running order before continuing—"because it seems to me that a man who is incapable of humor is capable of cruelty. If Hitler, for example, had had the ability—

116

the detachment—to observe the absurdity of his own behavior he would have laughed, and today there might not be a madman named Adolph Hitler."

Was he making a comparison between Hitler and my father? "Do you think my father is like that? Like Hitler?"

Anton looked thoughtful. "Cruelty is after all cruelty, and the difference between the two men may have more to do with their degrees of power than their degrees of cruelty. One man is able to affect millions and the other only a few. Would your father's cruelty cause him to crush weak neighboring states? Or would the *Führer's* cruelty cause him to beat his own daughter? Doesn't it seem to you that they both need to inflict pain?"

"I don't know."

Anton smiled. "I don't know either. But you see, the only questions I like to raise are those that are unanswerable. Trying to calculate the different degrees of cruelty is a lot like trying to calculate the different degrees of death."

I laughed, but I knew that tonight while our house slept I would stay awake trying to understand his words. "I'm so glad you're talking to me, teaching me." I heard my enthusiasm running over. "I want you to teach me everything you've learned."

Anton stood, executing a princely bow. "I'm at your service."

"I think I want to be intelligent even more than I want to be pretty."

"You're already intelligent and pretty."

"Me?"

"You. I come from a line of men who have a sure instinct for a woman's beauty. So, P.B., I speak as an expert when I tell you you're going to have it all."

"Well, why hasn't anyone else seen it? That I'm going to have—what you say?"

"They will. Because you are no common garden flower—you are unique."

"Oh."

"I think I'm going to enjoy being your teacher if you'll keep in mind that life produces no maestros, only students of varying degrees of ineptitude. Wait!" said Anton. He jumped from his chair to go rummaging through a GI regulation duffel bag. "Here it is!" He waved a book with a bruised, blue cover. "I checked it out of the prison library the same day I checked myself out. R.W. Emerson. Are you familiar with his work?"

I admitted that I wasn't while I wondered if escaping with a book could be called anything besides stealing. My father would never do anything like that.

Anton asked, "Is something wrong?"

"Uhhh, no. Well, I was wondering how you are going to return the book."

"Oh," he said thoughtfully. "You want to know if I am a thief?"

"Oh, no! I know you're not!"

"In this classroom we call things by their rightful name. I became a thief when I took that book. I couldn't very well pay for it, and I didn't want my brain to starve if I had to go into hiding."

I felt close to laughing. "You're very honest. I mean you don't lie, do you?"

Anton shook his head. "I try never to lie to myself, and I dislike lying to friends." He took a yellow pencil from his hip pocket and made two small check marks in R.W. Emerson's Table of Contents. "Read these essays," he said, like he felt pleased to be making a contribution to my education. "And tomorrow we can start mining the gold."

Then a voice from below us called up, "Come on folks! It's ready." Anton's face was caught in a moment of fear.

"It's all right," I whispered. "That's only Ruth, our housekeeper. She's made griddle cakes for us."

He looked at me. "Why did you—tell?"

He believed—he actually believed—that I would. "But I didn't! Honest! Ruth saw you run out of the garage last night; she saw how you wanted to protect me from my father."

Anton's hand rushed to his forehead. "I came running out of hiding to—My God, I did, didn't I?" His hand dropped to his side, and I could see he was smiling his wonderful glad-to-be-living smile. "After almost two years of being as inconspicuous a coward as possible I had no idea that I would voluntarily risk my life for anyone." He shook his head in disbelief. "But I'm glad I could. I'm glad I still could."

12

A PLAYFUL BREEZE brought a scent of roses into the breakfast room where it mingled with the purely kitchen aroma of coffee perking, griddle cakes rising, and bacon frying. The table was set for two with real cotton napkins, the newest of the everyday tablecloths, and our fancy dinnertime *made-in-Japan* china.

Ruth pointed to the chair where my father always sits, and Anton sat down. His appetite was healthy, and while we ate I heard Ruth singing in the kitchen: "Rinso white, Rinso white, happy little washday song."

She came into the breakfast room carrying the percolator and refilled the empty cups. Anton rose, pulling out a third chair. "Come join us." I watched Ruth's face for signs of embarrassment, for I was sure no white man had ever before offered her a chair. But if there was any, Ruth has better camouflage than the United States Army.

"Mr. Reiker, don't you worry none about me. I jest enjoys cooking for folks who enjoy eating." There it is! That's one of the things that Ruth does that makes the white ladies say she's uppity. All the other colored folks would have called him Mr. Anton, leaving the poor whites the privilege of calling him Mr. Reiker. But then, if Ruth played the piano I think she'd play only the cracks between the keys. She seems best suited for walking that thinnest of lines between respectfulness and subservience.

After a while Ruth brought in a cup of coffee and made herself comfortable in the chair that Anton had selected for her. Looking over at him, she chuckled. "Yes, sir, it is a pleasure to cook for folks who enjoys their food. They sure ain't no eaters in this house. Not Sharon and not—" she threw a nod over in my direction—"this child. She'd rather be sitting with me shelling peas than eating them. Mr. Bergen, he'd rather be left alone with his cigarettes, and Miz Bergen says she's gotta watch her girlish figure. Imagine that!" said Ruth. "A woman that bore two children wants a figure like some young girl's. I always tells her—a fruit-bearing tree knows better'n try to look like some young sapling."

Anton laughed. "You've been talking to my mother. Except she would have quoted the Bible, 'To every thing there is a season, and a time to every purpose under the heaven.' "

"A time to be born," supplied Ruth. "And a time to die."

Soon Ruth and Anton found a second point of agreement—that a good cook needs an appreciative eater or two. Then Ruth asked something a little surprising. It was something that she might have wondered out loud to me, but not to any other white person.

"How do they treat the colored folks there in Germany?"

"There aren't any."

Ruth's face slowly turned incredulous. "Then how do you folks keep your houses clean?"

I watched Anton laugh without making a sound. "The German housewife treats dirt as her mortal enemy. Anyway, our houses are fine; it's our politics and hearts that give us the trouble."

"It ain't only in your country, Mr. Reiker, no, sir! We've got plenty bad hearts right here in America.

When I was jest a girl I 'members my mamma saying, 'Things gonna be a lot better for my Ruth. My Ruth's smart and she's gonna grow up to be a teacher.' But my mamma was wrong. She didn't figger on them bad hearts. No, sir. And Mr. J.G. Jackson's daddy was one of them."

Ruth's eyes rolled downward to the sun-speckled linoleum floor. "He's gone on his reward now, Mr. Eugene Jackson. Well, back then he used to keep my mamma's savings for her in his office safe. Every Saturday for so many years my mamma would go into Mr. Jackson's office in the back of the cotton gin with fifty or seventy-five cents in her hand and tell him, 'Put this in the envelope, Mr. Jackson. Put this away, please, for my girl's education.' Well, when the time come for me to go away to teacher's school, there weren't but three dollars and twenty-five cents in that envelope."

Is it possible that the rich would steal from the poor? Why hadn't she ever told me that story before? After all, that was my friend Edna Louise's grandfather. "Ruth, how come you never told me before about what Mr. Jackson did to you?"

" 'Cause telling bad stories 'bout the dead ain't the best way to be spending time, and I ain't proud of myself even if I did jest tell it for purposes of illustration."

Then almost on signal we all began silently to watch the white dotted swiss curtains respond to the gentle change in the wind. The breakfast room was filled with lazy warmth, and I wondered if there was any better place to be than here. Here with my two favorite people getting to know each other.

Though after a while when you start to feel more the hardness of the chair than the softness of its cushion it would be good if just the two of us could get up and take a walk together down Main Street. I'd introduce him as my good friend, Anton. Anton Reiker.

And when he'd look back at me and smile everybody would see, plain as day, that this beautiful man really liked me.

Ruth's spoon sounded against the saucer beneath her cup. "When I had my boy, my Robert," she looked over at Anton. "He's 'bout your age now. I said, like my mamma before me said, 'Things gonna be different for my child 'cause I ain't gonna save no money in no white man's private safe, no, sir!' I put it all in the Rice County National Bank where Mr. John Rusk marked down every deposit in a little blue book. And so one fine day I saw my dream come true.

"On that day just before the sun come up Claude and me walked Robert down to the railroad station. And in his hand Robert was carrying all his things in a suitcase the church had given him the Sunday before. When they flagged down the Atlanta train, the one that was gonna take him to Morehouse College, I pulled out my handkerchief and Robert said, 'Don't you cry none, Ma. I leave here only a man, but I'm gonna come back to you a true minister of God.'

"And he would have been too 'cepting for the letter he got a few precious months later from Mr. Price Cook, the head man of the draft board. I went right down to Cook Brothers' Furniture and Appliances store and I 'plained to him how this is Robert's one chance in this world and I begged him to just let my boy finish up his schooling, let him become a true minister of the gospel. 'Ruth, I'm surprised at you,' he told me. 'You oughta know I can't do that. Why, this is your boy's country too and he's gotta do his share so this country will always belong to us Americans.' "

Funny, but Ruth never talked like that to me. Oh, sometimes she says just enough of something to let me know it is all a lie what the white folks keep saying. That lie they tell each other so often that they come to believe it's true: "I understands these niggers; they're happy and they don't know no better."

"Mr. Reiker." She called his name slowly, thoughtfully. "You're a smart man. I was wondering, do you reckon that this here world is ever gonna amount to much?"

"Call me Anton. Well, I'm not exactly overburdened by excessive optimism. For centuries men have believed that religion is the answer." Ruth, as if by instinct, clutched the gold cross at her throat. "But I have seen the evil perpetrated by religious men. Did you know that before every battle Hitler calls upon God for victory?"

Anton paused to make sure his point had sunk in. "A lot of people today believe education can save the world. I used to believe that, but I became discouraged while watching the educated Germans express their enthusiasm for this war. To give you an example," he said, looking from Ruth to me, "would one of you ask me what is the oldest tradition of the proud University of Göttingen?"

"What is their oldest tradition?" I asked, feeling like a parrot.

"Dueling. The *landsmannschaft!*" He stopped short like he had just run into a snag. "I don't know if you have anything like this in your country or not. It's a secret society. The word means 'clan.' "

"We have the Klan, sure do," responded Ruth.

"Well, the *landsmannschaften* would challenge each other to a duel on any pretext," Anton continued. "Sometimes even the narrow sidewalk of Göttingen was disputed by students from opposing clans. It's called 'defending their honor.' "

"I think maybe good changes will come when our leaders are better and there aren't any more evil dictators," I said.

Anton nodded. "There are those who would agree with you. But leaders don't usually spring forth to impose their will upon a helpless people. They, like department stores, are in business to give people what they

124

think they want. So basically you always come back to people. How do you make better people?"

"I believes," said Ruth, "the Lord himself would be mighty interested in creating better people. But if the Lord already knows how to do it then I don't, so you jest tell me."

"Maybe psychiatry?" I offered. "I read in the *Readers' Digest* where lots of people are helped to be better by psychiatry."

Anton's lips pressed together. "Maybe. Maybe not."

"Why can't you believe it?" I challenged. "The *Readers' Digest* wouldn't say it if it wasn't so."

Anton grinned. He looked like a charter member of *Our Gang Comedy*. "Maybe you're right, but maybe, just maybe, we all have an enormous capacity for believing in anything that will provide us with a bit of comfort." Anton caught Ruth's eye. "Haven't you found this to be true?"

"I'll tell you the truth, Mr. Rei—Anton. Yes, sir, I've found this here a cold world, a mighty cold world, and a man and a woman, well, they needs a little comforting 'fore they freeze to death."

"I can't argue with that," said Anton heavily, as though conceding to Ruth.

"You don't believe in religion or education or psychiatry," I said, holding up three fingers. "Is there anything at all you do believe in?"

"Of course." Anton raised the coffee to his lips and when he replaced the cup, it was empty. "I believe that love is better than hate. And that there is more nobility in building a chicken coop than in destroying a cathedral."

Ruth nodded in affirmation. "Ain't it the truth."

Suddenly I heard the crunch of driveway gravel over the low hum of a car motor. Ruth clasped her heart. "Mr. Bergen! Lordy, it's him! Hide him, Patty, under your bed! Quick!"

As I led Anton to my bedroom I squeezed his hand so he'd know we would never betray him. Anton's hand left mine as he slid under the maple bed.

Out in the driveway a voice called Ruth's name. A woman's voice! I cautiously lifted one slant of the venetian blind to see Mrs. Henkins, little Sue Ellen's mother, protruding her beauty parlor coiffure out of the car window. "Is it O.K. to take Sharon to Wynne City with us? I have to buy Sue Ellen a pair of tap dancing shoes."

"Yes, Miz Henkins, I reckon it'll be O.K. What time you figgering on returning?"

I didn't hear Mrs. Henkins' answer, but the car backed down the driveway and took off in the direction of Wynne City.

In the breakfast room we three sat totally absorbed in watching agitated curtains being egged on by a suddenly gusty wind. It was as though we were all waiting for something to happen.

After a while, Anton spoke. "About what happened—I'm sorry. There's no reason why you both should have to take risks. Tonight when it's dark I'll go."

"I'll pack you up some food to take with you," said Ruth with unaccustomed speed. "And I have a couple of dollars and some change you can have."

Did she realize what she was saying? Did she understand that he meant to leave us for good? "We're not afraid of anything, really. And it's not safe for you to leave here. They're all looking for you, Anton. Tell him, Ruth. Tell him!"

But Ruth didn't say anything. She got up from her chair, letting her eyes sweep across the table as she picked up the empty coffee cups and carried them off to the kitchen.

13

FROM OVER AT the button factory the five o'clock whistle blew, which didn't mean a thing since quitting time wasn't for another hour. I leaned back against the front stoop and tried to come up with the logic behind a five o'clock whistle.

But two men were all that I could think of. If I ever had to sacrifice one for the other which one would it be? The one who had fed and sheltered me, or the one whom I had fed and sheltered?

Sharon came out the front door, clutching her Baby Jane doll by the hair. Sharon, pretty Sharon, if I had been born that pretty maybe they would like me as much as her. And she's going to be about as popular as Betty Grable. My father says that in a few years, "the boys will be swarming about, thick as flies."

She sat down. "My baby has a boo-boo." Sharon pointed to a dark smudge on the doll's forehead.

"Rock your baby in your arms," I told her, "and tell her that you love her."

Sharon swayed back and forth and in a small voice began to chant: "I love you, little baby, I love you little baby. I love you, love you, love you, little baby."

Six o'clock came before my thoughts had congealed into plans. My father's green Chevy pulled into the driveway and stopped inside the garage. How close were the two men now? In yards, feet, and inches, exactly how far above my father is Anton? Funny, but with just a little information from me my father could achieve an instant acceptance in this town. The kind that he has wanted all his life. And it would only take one phone call: "Hello? Sheriff Cauldwell? . . . Yes, this is Harry Bergen. I've got your Nazi . . . . Yes, he's hiding in the rooms above my garage. Now here's what I want you to do . . . ."

Mr. Harry Bergen, prominent local merchant. His picture would be in all the newspapers. The President, or J. Edgar Hoover at the very least, would pin a medal on him, and the Jenkinsville Rotarians would call him a hero.

And then one evening after all the commotion had died down, I'd be sitting alone on the screened-in porch. In the twilight he'd come out and without saying a word, he'd sit beside me on the metal glider. After a while he'd casually drop his arm around my shoulder and say, "I haven't been much of a father, have I?"

It would take me a couple of swallows before I could manage to say, "Oh, you've been all right, really."

We'd just sit there for a while longer not saying anything. Every once in a while, though, he'd give my arm a couple of gentle pats to show how much he appreciated my help in apprehending the dangerous Nazi. Then probably he'd remark what a hot night it was, and maybe we ought to take a walk to the drug store for a cold Dr Pepper. "Oh, I'd like that, Daddy, I really would."

From inside the house I heard Ruth calling us to supper. I stood up and wondered how to go about starting from the very beginning. All the bad things were in the past. This is now and I am his daughter and he will love me. They say Jesus lived a truly perfect life. If I tried, really tried, I too could be perfect, or at the very least, sweet like Sharon. As my hand reached out for the door, I saw Sharon's Baby Jane doll lying face down beneath the rainspout. "And I love you, love you, love you, little baby."

I sat down at my place, but immediately jumped up and cheek-kissed both my mother and father before sitting down again. Look at him now. Be sweet. "Hey, that's an awfully nice tie you're wearing, is it from the store?" He said it was. A compliment about the store, maybe that would please him more. "That sign you put up over the shoe department—the large red one that says, SHOE DEPARTMENT. What a good idea! Is it good for business?"

His head was bent. "Eat your dinner and don't ask so many questions."

"But did you know that this doctor from Boston, I read it somewhere, said pleasant conversation is good for the digestive system?"

"And I told you to shut up and eat your dinner!" His anger ended my flirtation with perfection. If there were questions or confusion before, they weren't there anymore. I knew what I was going to do, and I knew why.

He lifted a fork overburdened with mashed potatoes, and I watched as the gravy started to roll down his chin. Across his mean, thin line of a mouth he smeared the paper napkin. It's not even a contest leaving you, dear Father. I know it will be difficult for you, deciding what to tell people, but will you miss *me*?

And what about you, Mother? Will I miss you? And do you love me? I only know for sure that we've never liked each other. Anyway it'll be easier loving you from a distance.

And Sharon. I'll love you no matter where I am. Sharon and Ruth, that's who I'll miss.

Ruth came out of the bathroom wearing her blue rayon walking-home dress, and at the bottom of the *V*-neck was the rhinestone pin in a flower design that I

129

gave her last Mother's Day. In a brown grocery sack she carried the cotton house dress that always got a washing and an ironing every time it got a wearing.

"I'll walk you a-ways," I offered.

When we reached Nigger Bottoms, Ruth said that it was getting on towards seven and I'd best be turning back. "Well, before I go," I said, wondering what I was going to say next, "I want to wish you a nice evening and—and good-bye."

Ruth smiled and wished me a pleasant evening. Then her forehead wrinkled up and I expected that I was in for some kind of warning. "Now, Honey Babe, I don't want you nowhere near that garage, you understand? Anton's gonna be leaving after dark, and it won't do nobody no good if the law catches him here. No Jewish girl and no colored woman needs that kinda trouble."

I hated seeing her so heavy with cares. "Ruth, you oughtna worry. This doctor in Boston says that worrying makes you feel old before your time."

"This here doctor from Boston you're always talking about," she said. "Did he say what you're 'pose to do with your burdens? They got pills in Boston for that?"

When she gets sarcastic there's not much I can think to say to her. But I didn't want to leave her like that. I guess I didn't want to leave her at all. "Well, now," I said, grabbing her hand, "you be good now." What a stupid, idiotic, last good-bye thing to say. Even for me. "Well, Ruth," I said, trying again. "Good-bye."

As I turned I caught a look on her face of surprise or suspicion. I walked on, feeling a painful pinching against the hollow of my stomach. "Well, see you tomorrow," I called out, and without even turning to look I knew her doubts were being laid to rest.

I found my bedroom in quiet shadows. I was aware of the room like you are when you look, I mean really look, at something for the first, or last, time. The twin maple beds with their matching yellow and blue chenille spreads, the linoleum with its pictures of the cat and the fiddle and the old lady in the shoe that had been a source of embarrassment for quite a few years now. I remember Edna Louise looking at that linoleum and saying, "I haven't liked Mother Goose in years."

The only thing that I really liked in my room was the desk my grandma had bought me. Inside was my simulated leather five-year diary. I wanted to record my life so I wouldn't forget anything, but then I discovered there wasn't much worth remembering.

For a while I tried to use my diary for self-improvement. I made three vertical columns down the page and marked the headings: DATE. CRITICISM. FROM WHOM. I thought if I could see them written down then correcting my shortcomings might not be all that difficult. I didn't have to wait long for my first entry. "5/15/41—7:35 A.M.: 'Get that hair out of your face.' —Mother. 5/15/41—7:45 A.M.: 'Even when you comb it, it doesn't look it. Can't you get that dirty hair out of your face?'—Mother."

Water began to drain noisily down the pipes. Sharon shrieked for a towel. Still time enough for packing. What did I need? Springy tennis shoes for jumping aboard slow-moving freight trains, polo shirts that never need ironing, blue jeans that save the legs from cockleburs, and a sweater for when the nights turn chilly. And, in case we go out together in some distant place, a dress.

In the bottom drawer of the kitchen cabinet Ruth stores dozens of neatly folded grocery sacks. I picked one for my suitcase and thought of Robert's suitcase, the one the whole church chipped in to buy him. How proud he must have felt—all those people wishing him well.

After the nine o'clock news was over, the big upright radio in the living room was snapped off, and

131

my mother and father began readying for bed. At nine thirty his breathing deepened into snores, and I guessed that my mother must be sleeping too. Sure she was. Haven't I heard him joke about it, "Pearl falls asleep on her way to the pillow."

The unhooked window screen pushed out with a sound so slight that I didn't bother to check to see if Sharon slept on. I dropped my paper bag to the ground and started to follow when I thought of something. I went over and stood for a moment by my sleeping sister.

Sharon lay curled on her side, just a small soft thing, her lips resting against her thumb. Already past the age when she needs to thumb-suck, but not yet ready to stop keeping it handy.

"Well, be good now," I said. "I sure hope you grow up nice." Sharon's reluctant eyes opened. She took hold of my hand and closed her eyes again. As I tried to loosen my hand she seemed to get a better grasp, like she didn't want me to go or maybe she didn't want me to go without her. "Want to come along?" I whispered. Groaning like her sleep was being disturbed, she released my hand and turned over.

Outside, the darkness was complete. I walked by the sandpile and the chinaberry tree whose strongest branch supported our chain swing. The seat had been cut from an old restaurant sign, and there was still the word, "EATS" painted in faded red letters.

Is this how it all ends? Leave everything you know, and all that comes to mind is trivia—sandpiles and chinaberries.

I left my sack at the foot of the garage steps and crawled my way up through the blackness. "Anton," I whispered. But behind the closed door, there was only silence. A feeling of loss swept over me. "Anton!" I cried, hitting the door with my fist. "It's me! Patty!"

Abruptly the door opened. "Quiet!" As he led me through the blackness I tried to find my voice. "I thought, I thought you had gone," I said and then from somewhere came crying. Only after my tongue had tasted saltiness did I know its source.

Anton squeezed my hand.

"I'm sorry," I said. "I didn't know I was going to do that."

Anton brought my hand to the slightly moist inner corners of his own eyes. "Just wanted to point out that the biggest difference between us is that you cry more noisily than I."

I laughed, feeling grateful for the darkness which concealed my eyes.

"We both knew that I couldn't stay. It had to happen, P.B., you always knew that."

"No, I didn't!" I breathed in deep. "Anton—" I needed to say his name aloud again as though it were a magical incantation. "Anton, I won't even be that much trouble. What I'm trying to tell you is—" The hurdle felt too high for vaulting.

"P.B., I don't think—"

"Don't talk. Listen to me." It was my hurdle, and I had to clear it myself. "I don't think you oughta leave me, not now. I haven't learned all those things you were going to teach me—things about Emerson and—and— Oh, Anton, let me be with you, go where you go."

His thumb pressed against my palm. "You know what you are asking is impossible, but if you're saying that you love me—"

"Yes," I answered, wondering if it came out audibly. "Yes."

"Then know this, Patty, it's not completely one-sided. I love you too, and in my own way I'll miss you."

He opened the door, climbed quickly down, and offered up his hand to me.

Outside, the moon, almost full-grown now, threw soft illumination on his forehead and cheeks while

133

leaving the deeper recesses in shadows. Then it struck me that if someday I grow old and forgetful, forgetting even friends' names and faces, his face I could never forget.

He looked down at the luminous hands of his watch. "The train comes by about ten fifteen."

"Yes," I replied and then, thinking that my answer sounded curt, I added, "Yes, it does."

"Let me help you back into the house," he offered. "There's still time."

I began to feel jealous of time and trivia. Of last moments consumed in pass-the-salt type of comments. "No thanks. My bedroom window screen is unhooked and the water spigot is there, makes a good foothold."

"Well, I must say good-bye now."

"Oh, I almost forgot." I dug into the right-hand pocket of my jeans. "Here's some money—only four dollars and sixty-five cents. It's all Ruth and I had."

He took the money. "Thanks for this, for everything. And I have something for you too. It belonged to my father and his father and even his father before that." Anton looked down at his hand. Then warm metal encircled my finger. "This ring was made by Germany's most famous goldsmith for my great-grandfather when he was president of the university of Göttingen. The crest represents the office of the president."

A thing of value! He'd give it to me? "Maybe you'd better keep it, Anton. I mean, it has been in your family for so long." My tongue! I could bite it off. The ring had been mine for only a moment, and now I would lose that too.

"The greater the value, the greater the pleasure in giving it. The ring is yours, P.B." Then in the darkened silence, I heard him breathe in deeply. "Am I still your teacher?" Without pausing for an answer he continued, "Then I want you to learn this, our last, lesson. Even if you forget everything else I want you to always remember that you are a person of value, and you have

134

a friend who loved you enough to give you his most valued possession."

"I will, Anton. I'll remember."

I saw or felt it coming—my chin tilted up as my eyes closed. Then our lips touched, lingered together briefly before going their own separate ways. When I opened my eyes Anton was gone.

Time passed. I stood rigid and unmoving, wanting nothing new to happen to me. New time was nothing except a way to determine how long he had been gone. From under the weight of my foot I felt a chinaberry being pushed into the damp ground. My finger passed over the indented crest of the gold ring.

Then from down the distant tracks came the ten fifteen.

14

FOR A WHILE I carefully kept track of time without Anton. One day, one day and a third, five days, seventeen. Then abruptly I stopped counting. For one thing I didn't like the time being long or the distance great. And marking off time struck me as something like counting empty spaces—spaces you know can't ever be filled.

"Patricia Ann." A voice came intruding into my world. "Do you find the schoolyard more interesting than our little problems in fractions?"

A classroom of heads turned to stare at me. Quick, answer the question. About fractions, was I interested in them?

"Oh, yes, ma'am," I said, trying to put real conviction in my voice. "Yes, ma'am, I sure do."

Miss Hooten's head tilted slightly to the right while Edna Louise led the class in snickering. "Are you sassing me, Patricia Ann?"

"Oh, no, ma'am, I only meant that I do like fractions, and I apologize for looking out the window."

While Edna Louise attempted to revive the snickering, Miss Hooten's face gradually relaxed. "Boys and girls, you have just heard a proper apology, and I hope that the next time any of you are called down that you will be able to do as well. Hear me talking, Edna Louise?"

It had to be a dream. Who would dare call Edna Louise Jackson down?

Edna Louise let out a wail. "I don't know why you're picking on me. I wasn't looking out the window." Her index finger pointed at me. "Patty was!"

I found myself focusing on that finger aimed at destroying me. You would never have loved her, Anton. Never given her your ring. Pulling the yellow chain up from around my neck, my fingers passed across the heavy crested ring. "Oh, you're weak, Edna Louise," I whispered to the ring. "And you're no person of value either."

Juanita Henkins between, "Well, uhs," was trying to remember the principal crops of Brazil when the three-fifteen bell sounded. "Saved by the bell!" called out one of the boys. C.J. Peters I think it was.

By the time I had walked the block to the store I had come to a decision—a ring of such power and beauty has no business being hidden away beneath some dress front. It should be worn proudly for all the world to see.

In the store there was a small gathering of people. From their backsides I recognized Gussie Fields, Sister Parker, my father, a couple of women customers, and my mother. They were all the approving audience of a single performer, little Sharon, who was dancing and prancing around as she sang: "They're either too young or too old. They're either too dull or too grassy green."

When she finished, Sharon dropped her head and gave her fans an adorable little curtsy.

"Oh, Honey," cried Gussie Fields, "that's just wonderful." She gave her boss a congratulating pat on the shoulder. "I didn't know such talent ran in your family. Bet she takes after you."

My father laughed and then, finding a remaining Lucky in a flattened pack, he said, "Now, Gussie Mae, you're gonna think I'm crazy when I tell you this, but to my mind Sharon is every bit as good as Shirley

Temple. And remember, Sharon hasn't had anywhere near the training that Shirley Temple has!"

"Mr. Bergen," said the clerk, "you're not one little bit crazy. No, sir! I'll tell you the truth. When I saw that child sing and dance in Sue Dobbins's dance recital, well, I said to myself right then and there she's got that special something—that movie-star sparkle, I guess you'd call it."

"I've never in my life told this to anyone before," said my father, pausing to blow out a blue-gray puff of smoke. Was he about to make a confession to Gussie? He mustn't see I'm listening. I bent down to tie a shoe-lace before realizing that I was wearing my brown loafers. "But one night, I sat up till almost midnight," he said, "thinking that I oughta take Sharon, now don't laugh, right out to Hollywood. All they'd have to do is to see her sing one of her little songs or do one of her cute dances. Well, in my opinion, it would put Jenkins-ville right on the map."

My sister a real name-in-lights movie star?

Sharon spotted me and came running over, pointing to her left elbow. "Look! It's skinned." What's she always bothering me for with her tiny scratches? Little big shot. My hand became a hard fist that wanted to ram itself into her pretty face.

In my meanest voice I said, "Why can't you just leave me alone?"

I ran to an out-of-sight place between counters stacked high with blue overalls and burrowed my head between two stacks of denims.

I felt something pressing into my chest bone—the ring! Pulling it up, I gave it a wet kiss before making a prayer–wish: "Oh, God, please don't ever let Anton find out that I was so hateful and mean. Help me to become a person of value."

Funny that I could forget about my ring. After all that's why I came into the store. I wanted a piece of tape to wrap around it.

Sister Parker dropped a jar of Royal Peach Hairdressing into a tan sack, handed it to a colored woman, and rang twelve cents on the cash register.

I asked, "Want me to help you do something?"

"Well," she said, "you can staple the candy bags closed if you want to."

More than a hundred cellophane bags of orange slices, chocolate-covered peanuts, and peppermint discs lay on the counter waiting for the staple gun. As I stapled, Sister tore open a fresh fifty-pound box of my favorite chocolate-covered malt balls.

"That'll make up into lots of sacks," I said.

"I reckon."

"About how many, do you think?"

After a long pause Sister said, "A lot, I know that."

I stopped my stapling, got pencil and paper, and in less than a jiffy came up with the answer. "Now you give one ounce to each sack, so that fifty pounds will make up into eight hundred sacks."

Sister Parker didn't say anything, so I asked, "Isn't that interesting?"

"I guess. It's interesting enough for folks who have nothing better to do than to think."

"But, Sister," I protested, feeling like Anton was here borrowing my voice for his thoughts. "A person's got to think, otherwise that person's no better than a trained seal balancing a ball on his nose. If only that seal could think, he'd know he was making a thousand children laugh."

"What do you want me to think about?" asked Sister, sounding more tired than unfriendly. "Eight hundred bags of candy?"

"Maybe you could think about eight hundred people who are going to enjoy the candy you sacked. After all, work should have relevance," I said, borrowing one of Anton's words.

My ring was dazzling me with its closeness and

139

its power. Sister seemed receptive (another of his words), so I decided to slide into the subject like it was the most natural thing in the world. I extended my left hand. "Did you see my ring?"

Sister looked up. "Did your boyfriend give it to you?"

"Boyfriend?" I asked, confused. "Who are you talking about?"

"Well, I don't know," she said. "You oughta know who your boyfriend is."

"It's a real solid gold ring." I dropped the ring into Sister's hand. "Feel the weight?"

"Where did you get it?" She was really interested all right.

"Well, I'll tell you the truth," I said, interested myself to know what the truth was going to be. "It happened on Monday. Now, I know for sure it was a Monday 'cause that was the day school started, you remember?"

Sister nodded.

"Well, as I was walking home from school, it was only about noontime. School let out early that day, remember?"

Sister answered with only a "Hmmm."

Then it came to me—my vision of the truth. "Well, I saw this man walking down the road. He looked like an old man 'cause of his whiskers—white whiskers. He asked me if I lived nearby and if I could spare a piece of bread with maybe a bit of butter on it.

"I took the man home and he sat on the back doorstep, and while Ruth was busy vacuuming the living room I kept bringing him our best food. Well, after the man finished eating he thanked me and said that because I was obviously a person of value he was going to reward me with his most valued possession. And so he slipped that very ring on my finger."

Sister Parker's hands had forgotten their work and her eyes looked slightly larger than I remembered. I

140

felt powerful, like I finally had something somebody else wanted even if it was only the rest of the story. Well, I'd give her an ending—a great motion picture ending.

"But it was what happened next that was the most surprising thing of all. I mean—" I said, stalling. "It was what he said next."

"What did he say?"

"He told me that he wasn't really poor. He only pretended to be to find all the good people in the world. He said that he gives his wife—want to know her name?"

"All right."

"Agnes. He said that Agnes could buy this whole town and everything that's in it with just the money he gives her weekly."

Sister began shaking her head. "Now tell me another."

I felt annoyance rising in me. "I guess you also don't believe that Jesus walked on water. I mean you don't seem to believe in anything unless you see it happen. Haven't you any faith?"

"I have faith, plenty of it. But, well, why don't you tell me the rest."

"All right, it might be helpful to you. The man told me that because I was able to show such good faith towards a stranger I would be rewarded on my eighteenth birthday. No matter where I might be, my present would reach me on that day."

"And this ring," said Sister, holding it between her fingers, "is yours for a remembrance?"

"Mine for a remembrance," I said, thinking of Anton. "You know, it's my most valued possession."

"Hey, Mr. Bergen," called Sister Parker across the store. "Is this ring really solid gold?"

"What? What are you talking about?" He strode over in his save-the-nation gait. "Whose ring is this?"

Sister looked surprised. I held hands with myself

to keep them steady. "Why it's Patty's—I guess it is."

I didn't say anything; my brain felt like Jell-O left too long in the heat. Why did I have to tell anybody? Why can't I keep my stupid mouth shut? He examined the ring by squinting his right eye and then his left one. Suddenly he jerked away the tape.

"Twenty-four carat," he said slowly. "Whose ring is this?"

"Mine—"

"How did you get it? Where'd it come from?"

"Well— You know how we got out of school early on Monday 'cause it was the first day of school?"

"Get to the point!"

My last year's dress suddenly felt too small. "I'm trying to tell you if you'll please be patient."

"You better tell me in one hell of a hurry!"

I noticed that the stuff that the drug store had sold him for those tobacco stains on his teeth wasn't helping. "Well," I said, "I met this man who asked me to give him some food because he was very, very hungry. I told him to follow me home, and he did, and he sat on the back doorstep while I brought him—you want to know what I brought him?"

I didn't see how my father responded because my eyes were fixed on the SHOE DEPARTMENT sign at the back of the store. "Bread and butter and some slices of American cheese—and I think two oranges." I forced myself to look him in the face. "And so—that's what happened," I concluded.

"What *happened?*"

What does he want from me? It isn't like him to get excited about a little cheese and a couple of oranges for a starving man.

"Are you gonna tell me!" His mouth smelled like yesterday's ash tray. "Tell me who he was."

"A man, a hungry man. I told you."

"White or colored?"

It wasn't the food that bothered him, but what?

142

"White," I said, hoping this would give him some reassurance. "He was white."

My father sucked in a deep breath. "How old was he?"

Where were we going? I searched Sister Parker's face for a clue, but the only thing I could see was interest and, maybe, fear. "He wasn't too young. He had whiskers that were turning gray; I guess he was at least forty."

"And this man, you gave him something too, didn't you?" My father's voice had become calm, almost confidential.

Then it came to me what this was all about. Sure. That must be it. I thought about the time I sneaked into the movies without paying and later when I told him about it, he made me go back with the money. He's a regular Abraham Lincoln. My confidence reappeared.

"Yes, sir," I said. "I sure did."

"What was it?"

Maybe he did care about the oranges, which might be kind of expensive, coming all the way from Florida. "I gave him what I told you. Bread and cheese and —and two little oranges that were overripe and about to go bad."

"What did he do to you?"

What does he want me to say? "The only thing he did was to thank me. He was very polite."

"You're lying, you dirty girl."

"No, sir, I'm telling the truth."

"Liar! He touched you. You let him put his hands on you, *filthy, fil-thy* girl!" As he raised his hand I clamped my eyes shut.

"Awww!" I fell backward against the magazine stand and slid down while a landslide of periodicals tumbled across my chest and legs.

As he walked away I spoke to his back. "And I don't love you. Nobody does!"

15

Sister Parker led me by the elbow toward the back of the store and then up the steps to the balcony. "You're gonna be all right," she said.

From below came my mother's voice. "What did she do? Why did you hit her? *Harry?*"

Sister guided me past large cartons of unopened merchandise and my father's polished pine desk to the brown studio couch. A couple of times a day my father whispers to my mother, "Watch out for things. I'm gonna go rest my eyes on the couch."

"Now lie down," said Sister. "I'll bring you a cold towel for your face." There? She wants me to lie down there where his head has rested?

"No, it's too soft. Here on the floor, where it's cool." Sister Parker stooped to place the couch's tired brown bolster under my head before turning to leave.

From downstairs I heard the rapid cranking of the phone. "Mary? Is the sheriff in his office? All right, then try his home. Hello? Sheriff Cauldwell? . . . This is Harry Bergen. I want you to come down to the store right now. . . . I don't know whether it is or not. Come over and find out." The receiver was slammed down.

"What did you call *him* for?" I heard my mother's voice go hysterical. "Harry, tell me what's wrong!"

"Nothing."

"Yes, something *is*."

"Damn you, woman, don't you go calling me a liar! Your mother may lead your old man around by the nose, but you're not gonna do it to me!"

Damn them! Damn them both! Must they let the whole world see them fight?

Where he hit me my face felt bruised and hot. My stomach, though, felt the worst. All the food I'd eaten, all the food I'd ever eaten, moaned and churned, growing putrid and decayed.

"Anton," my voice whispered, "why did you have to go and leave me?" Hiccupy sobs came to keep company with my body shakes. God, I wish I could shut up and sink deep and unnoticed into the ground. Die. Yes, die with the mark of his hand still across my face. Explain that to people, to the sheriff, to the judge.

Outside, a car made a sudden attention-getting stop, and within moments I recognized the guns-and-bullets voice. "What's up, Harry?"

My brain felt too bruised to even think about a plan. How long did I have? Not very. Remembering my source of strength, my right hand went rushing across left fingers. Then I remembered that I didn't have it anymore. I didn't have my ring!

Footsteps, like cannons, ascended the balcony stairs. Beat me! Kill me! Not one thing am I going to say till I get back my ring. "Remember," Anton had said to me, ". . . you have a friend who loved you enough to give you his most valued possession."

The footsteps stopped at my head and for a moment all was quiet. Then my father broke the silence. "Get yourself off that floor." As I rolled over on my stomach he spoke again. "The sheriff is here. There's a lot of things he wants to know. Do ya hear?" I stood up and looked him in the eye.

"Answer me!"

The words struck wounds that hadn't even begun to heal and the crying started anew.

145

"Go on downstairs. Let me talk to her, Harry," said the big voice.

"Talk to her," said my father. "Go on, but I'm gonna stay right here."

"Now, Patty, we've been knowing each other for quite a long spell now." The big voice was speaking softly. "And you're a smart girl, and I respect that. I want you to respect the fact that I'm a big old two-hundred-and-fifty-pound sheriff who'd never raise his hand against you."

"Ask the questions," demanded my father.

"Harry, which one of us is the sheriff of this here county? If you let me be the sheriff then I'm gonna let you be the merchant." Sheriff Cauldwell sat me down on the couch and he settled into my father's desk chair. "Patty, if some man did something to hurt you, you gotta tell me about it so I can stop him. So that he can never do it again to some other young girl. Now, you tell me, Patty, 'cause you ain't got a thing to be afraid of."

I looked past the sheriff's elbow to see if my father had disintegrated. He hadn't. "Sheriff Cauldwell, please, may I have my ring back now?"

"Why, shore you can. Harry, give her back her ring."

"I'm keeping it for evidence."

"You being the sheriff again, are you? Give Patty back her ring."

I heard the air rushing like a powerful vacuum through my father's nostrils. I prayed that if God wouldn't protect me, surely Sheriff Cauldwell would. One, two, three, four, five, six, seven, eight, nine, ten. I opened my eyes to see my ring pass from my father's fingers to the sheriff's and finally back into my waiting hand.

"Oh, thanks. Is it mine to keep? Is anybody going to take it away from me?"

Sheriff Cauldwell turned a steady gaze on my

146

father. "Anybody touches that ring gonna have to answer to me first. Now, you want to tell me where you got it?"

"Yes, sir. There was this man—he was kinda old 'cause his whiskers were white—and he told me that he hadn't eaten in quite a while. So I told him that if he would follow me home and sit on our back doorstep I'd bring him some food from our refrigerator. And so I did and so he gave me the ring."

The sheriff rubbed his chin. "Did anything else happen? I mean, did he hurt you in any way?"

"Oh, no, sir."

"Well, did he touch you anywhere on your body?"

"Oh, no, sir. Except—"

"Except what?" Something of the guns-and-bullets quality returned to his voice.

"Except when we touched hands to shake good-bye."

Sheriff Cauldwell released a low chuckle, shaking his head. "And that's all there was to it, huh? Where was your colored woman when you were feeding this man?"

"Well, she was in the house, cleaning the living room, I think. But she didn't know anything about his being there."

The sheriff was looking at me with his heavy, yet strong-jawed face, and I got to liking him, this man of power who didn't like to hurt. "And you're saying your colored woman was close enough that if you hollered she'd have heard you and come a-running?"

"Oh, yes, sir! She would have run so fast—Ruth wouldn't let anybody hurt me."

Sheriff Cauldwell let out a deep sigh. "Well, now, Harry, I'm gonna tell you; I'm real satisfied. You?"

"No, I'm not." My father's voice sounded stretched, like rubber bands, to the breaking point. "I'm a long way from being satisfied. Why'd he give her the ring, can you answer me that? Twenty-four carat gold?"

"I reckon I'm not above asking. Why did he give you the ring, Patty?"

"Well, I mean, you want to know the real reason?" I asked, waiting for my brain to send forth some kind of message.

"Yep," said Sheriff Cauldwell.

I rubbed the ring's indented crest across my lips and waited for its powers to surge forth. "Well, I suppose it's what he said to me after eating the food—" Then the reason came to me, dropping like a highly accurate weapon into my shooting hand. I turned and aimed it directly at my father. " 'Patty,' said the old man, 'I could go through this world proud and happy if only God had seen fit to give me a daughter exactly like you.' "

16

THE SUMMER OF my Anton was gone; fall was here and winter was coming. It felt like the right time to add up the gains and subtract the losses.

My losses were only one, only him. And yet that far outdistanced any gains. My fingers held his ring while my eyes explored, for an uncountable time, the mysteries of its princely crest.

There has been something to the good, I guess, because somehow it's different with my father. He sees me differently, maybe with more power. Yes, that's it! I tried to remember how it came to be and at what moment. I only knew that it was there, unmistakably there. The new ingredient wasn't love, it wasn't as good. It was, I guess, respect. Respect for a person who he's incapable of destroying.

I thought of last April when the tornado came roaring through town like the Missouri Pacific, taking with it the roof on Mr. McDonald's dairy barn. Tommy McDonald himself told me how all eleven of the milking cows were hurt except for the one which was outright killed. Only one animal, Esmeralda, a ten-year-old striped cat with one eye, survived intact.

And that's what he didn't know before. He knows that I'm an Esmeralda too for, whatever he may say or do, I'm going to survive pretty much intact. One gain.

Then there's my mother. Any gains there? Same

mother with the same little hit-the-victim-and-run comments. But now at least it's not my hair. She has a newer one: "How come Edna Louise has all the friends?" Just being in the same room with you, Mother, is like being feast for a thousand starving insects.

Tally it up: one loss, one gain, and one tie score.

From Anton's hide-out I watched a random leaf from a sturdy oak cut its family ties and float free on a small current of air.

Wish I were like that leaf. Someday, when the time is ripe, I'll soar away on my own air current. At eighteen the law says a person is no longer a child, and I'll have graduated from high school. Then there's the war bond, the one whole thousand-dollar war bond that Grandma and Grandpa Fried bought for me. Did they say for my college education? I don't remember. Well, what if they did? A person can do whatever she wants with her own money.

How far is it? And how much does it cost? A thousand dollars must be money enough, yes, of course, I can do it. But why didn't I think of it before? Suddenly I felt as though I had something to look forward to.

Something that I had once said to Sister Parker now seemed to carry the seeds of prophecy. That story I told about the ring and the man who promised me I would be rewarded on my eighteenth birthday. Could a made-up story carry a prophecy?

It was the most natural thing in the world. The war would be over by then, and surely for Anton I could grow at least a little beautiful. And Greyhound buses go to New York and boats to Germany and trains to Göttingen. Six more years isn't tomorrow—but it isn't forever either. I'd be eighteen and grown-up with gentle curves and long shiny hair. My hand felt some of the remaining brittle handiwork of Mrs. Reeves, and I remembered what Ruth is always saying, "Folks keep forgetting that wishing don't make nothing so, but prayer sometimes do."

"Oh, Lord," I called out like he had suddenly grown hard of hearing, "please give me long beautiful hair for him to love, Amen." And then as an afterthought, "And a bosom." My hand struck across the flat terrain of my chest. "I want a bosom of my very own!" Then it hit me that what I had asked for might come under the heading of blasphemy, so I quickly added, "If it's not too much trouble. I mean if it's O.K. with you that I should have one—I mean two."

"Patty! Oh-de-ho-ho, Patty!" Ruth always had this way of making a call from the back porch sound like a little song. She was waiting for me with a put-upon look. "How come he's a-coming home this time a day? What does he want to see you fer?"

"Who's coming home? Who wants to see me?"

"Him. Your daddy."

"But I haven't done anything!" I looked into Ruth's face, but the only thing there was a reflection of my own confusion. "Did he sound mad?"

Ruth's face registered mild surprise. "No. Not any madder than usual."

Then tension gushed from my body like air from a punctured inner tube. "He just wants me to do something for him, don't you think?"

Ruth nodded in agreement. "Now, whatever he wants done, you jest shake your head and tell him, 'Yes, sir.' You hear me talking to you, girl?"

I gave Ruth a half nod.

"And if you knows of a faster way, or a cheaper way, or even a nicer way, you jest keeps that information to yourself. He don't wanna hear nothing like that from you."

Annoyed, I answered, "I know all that." Yet, I was grateful for the reminder. I gave my ring a kiss for luck. "You don't suppose Sheriff Cauldwell told my father

151

that he could take my ring away, do you?" Then I answered my own question. "The sheriff wouldn't do such a thing. Besides, this is the most valuable thing I own. It's like—like my Bible, know that?"

"It tells one of them same stories the Bible do, love thy neighbor."

I pulled the ring from my finger, dropping it into the pocket of Ruth's apron. "Well, nobody's going to take it from me, not as long as I live."

From the distance of two blocks I heard the motor of the car gun itself up like it was just beginning the journey of a thousand miles, all up mountain. I didn't want him to think he had me concerned, so I grabbed a copy of the *Readers' Digest* and belly-dived to the bed.

The front door opened and slammed shut. I heard the sound of his voice without catching his words. But Ruth's voice came through unmistakably clear: "In her room, I reckon."

As the door swung open my eyes continued keeping company with the *Readers' Digest*. A rattle from a throat sent my gaze towards the door. Two men. And my father too. What do they want? *Danger!*

One of the men took a step forward. "Well, young lady, I'm Mr. Pierce. Remember me?"

Yes, so that's who it is. "No sir," I lied.

"Well, I just stopped by to chat."

"You tell him everything he wants to know," said my father, "or so help me you're gonna wish you'd never been born."

"Lots of time I wish that," I said in a normal voice, surprised that my thoughts came out in hearable words.

"God damn you, girl," he said, his face fired with sudden redness. "Who in hell do you think you're talking to?"

Mr. Pierce looked shocked or frightened or both. "Now, Mr. Bergen, please. She's only a kid."

I watched my father's face change to a color that more closely resembled purple "A kid! Now, you listen

here, Mr. FBI"——he pointed a trembling finger at me——
"that's no little kid, never has been, 'cause when she
was born her brain was bigger than yours is now. Understand?"

Was it possible that he was actually giving me a
compliment?

Mr. Pierce's ears seemed to catch my father's color-
ing. "I fail to understand what insulting me has to do
with the matter at hand?"

"I wasn't insulting you, I was warning you. You just
be careful of that girl, she can make lies sound like the
truth and the truth sound like a pack of vile lies. But
no matter how she lies, she wouldn't spit on a Nazi if
his body was on fire."

Pierce nodded. "Let's get on with it. I'd like to ask
your daughter a few questions."

"So question. Question!"

Pierce took out a gold fountain pen from his breast
pocket and opened a stenographic pad to a clean page.
"Tell me," he said after a pause, "what grade are you
in?"

"Seventh," I said, relieved at the way the questions
began. I'd feel even more relief if I knew what this was
about.

"Who are your teachers?"

"Teachers? I only have one," I said. "Miss Hooten,
unless you—do you want to know who my study hall
teacher is?"

"All right," he answered.

All right he did or all right he didn't? I had the feeling I shouldn't make any mistakes. "Do you want me
to tell you?"

"Yes."

"Coach Rawlings," I said as Mr. Pierce wrote something in his pad. "But he's not my teacher or anything.
We can go to the library on Fridays and read or study,
and he just sits there and keeps the kids quiet." I knew
I was making too much of it.

Pierce looked up from his pad. "You have a lot of friends?"

"Well, I guess so," I answered, grateful my mother wasn't here to contradict.

"Name them," said Pierce.

"Well," I said, thinking of Anton and Ruth, "they're just kids."

"Who are they?"

"Well, there's Edna Louise Jackson, she's one of my friends." I wondered if Edna Louise would ever list me as one of her friends. "And Juanita Henkins, and I guess, Donna Rhodes. I guess those are my main friends."

"Anybody else?"

I thought of good-old-raggedy-old Freddy Dowd who couldn't be mentioned in my father's presence. "No, sir, that's about all."

Mr. Pierce looked down. "Patricia, did you within the last five months give food to some tramp, somebody that you'd never seen before?"

It was plain he'd been talking to the sheriff and now he wanted to find out if the tramp could be Anton. "Yes, sir, I sure did."

"Tell me about it."

"Well, sir, during the summer I met this man and he looked an awful lot like a tramp and he told me that he hadn't eaten in—I forgot how long. Is it important? Should I try to remember?"

"Just go on with the story," said Pierce.

"Anyway, he asked if I could spare him some food and I told him that I could. And so I did—give him some food from our fridge. Is that what you want to know?"

"What was his name?"

I shook my head. "He didn't tell me."

"What was he wearing?"

"Just some old clothes that weren't clean."

154

"What did he look like?"

"He didn't look like anything too special. He looked tired 'cause his eyes had this redness like he hadn't been getting enough sleep."

"About how old would you say he was?"

"Well—" I began conjuring up my original vision of the tramp, the one I had used for Sister Parker and Sheriff Cauldwell. "He wasn't too young, some of his whiskers were getting grey. He may even have been forty, as old as that."

"Anything of a special nature that you noticed about the tramp?"

"Well, if there was any one thing I guess I'd have to say it was his politeness. He thanked me for every bit of food that I brought him."

Then Pierce asked his height, but before I had finished telling him that he wasn't too tall the FBI man was off on another question. "Did he talk like people from these parts?"

"Well, sir—" As he deliberately speeded up his questions, I deliberately slowed down my answers. "I'm not sure that he did."

The other FBI man led my father from the room saying something that sounded like, but it couldn't be, "Show me your clothes."

"How did he talk different?"

"Well, for one thing, he had polite manners."

"You told me that. I want to know about his accent. Did he, for example, sound like a Southerner?"

"No, sir, I really don't think so."

Pierce picked up a briefcase at his feet. "Where do you think he came from?"

"New York," I said automatically before even deciding whether it could do any harm. How could that help the FBI? After all, Anton wasn't from New York. Still, I felt uneasy.

Pierce slipped a glossy black-and-white photograph

from his briefcase. "Is this the tramp?" he asked, placing the picture before me.

It was him. Anton! "Sir?"

"I asked you if this man was the tramp?"

"Well, sir—." I said, not really sure of what to say. I couldn't quite figure out if it would hurt or help Anton if the FBI believed he was the tramp.

"Surely, you know whether or not this was the tramp. You gave him food; he gave you his ring. Why aren't you wearing it?"

"I lost it."

Pierce struck the photograph with his finger. "Well, is it him?"

I held the photo close and then out to arm's length. Ideas crashed head-on into other ideas. One idea revived itself: Make Mr. Pierce believe that I want to help him. "Well, Mr. Pierce," I said, finding his eyes. "It sure doesn't look too much like him, although, it could be if he were wearing a disguise. Do you think he wore a disguise?"

He answered my question by asking rapid-fire questions of his own. How did the tramp look like the picture? How did he not look like it? Eyes? Hair? Same or different? How? Why? Moles? Birthmarks? Clothes? Where did the tramp say he was going? Where had he been?

My head began to fog up. "Did you give the tramp any clothes to wear?" How much longer can this go on? Will there be a point when there are no more questions left to ask? Stay calm. Important, staying calm and pretending to be helpful. After all, how can I hurt Anton? I don't know where he is. He never told me where he was going. Yet, in my mind's eye I always saw him in New York City walking down Fifth Avenue, maybe even wearing an ascot from some fancy store.

Suddenly, something blue was pulled from the briefcase. "Do you recognize this shirt?" asked Pierce.

It was the Father's Day present. Near the shoulder was a tear, but it was still the shirt because on the pocket remained the initials, H.B.

"Well, do you?"

Anton ought to know better than to leave it lying around for people to find. "I may have seen it before, but I'm not sure. One shirt looks pretty much like another to me."

"You've seen this shirt before. Your daddy told me you bought it for him." Pierce picked up Anton's picture and waved it before my eyes. "And then you gave it to this man. This prisoner of war."

"Sir?"

"You heard every word I said!" He shoved the garment into my hands. "Look at it and tell the truth."

The tear was not so much a tear as a hole, quarter-sized, with purple stains smeared around it and two thick blotches of stain below. It was exactly the color you would expect to see if you mixed the blue of the shirt with the color red.

"Blood?" I waited for Pierce's denial. "Looks a little like blood." In a moment he would explain that it was only catsup stains. As I waited I searched his face, which was firmly set.

"Blood? *Blood!*" I screamed. "Did you hurt him?"

Pierce's face unset, and I knew that good news was coming. I waited for him to tell me that it was nothing serious—a few scratches across his chest.

Pierce's lips parted. He allowed himself the smallest of smiles. "Is who hurt?"

"You know who! The shirt's person."

"What's his name?"

"Reiker!" I shouted. "Frederick Anton Reiker. Is he going to be all right?"

I heard a noise that sounded like the sweet breath of satisfaction. Pierce took out a yellow half sheet of paper from his briefcase and read:

FREDERICK ANTON REIKER WAS SHOT EARLY THIS
MORNING WHILE TRYING TO AVOID ARREST. HE
DIED AT 10:15 A.M. IN NEW YORK'S BELLEVUE
HOSPITAL.

What was Pierce saying? Making jokes? Then it
struck me that the agent wasn't laughing and wasn't going to, for what he said wasn't meant to be a joke. Yet,
it couldn't be true. His words came back to me—at
10:15 A.M. Frederick Anton Reiker died in New York's
Bellevue Hospital.

The alarm clock on the night table ticked out the
seconds. A cry like from a wounded animal scattered
the quiet for what seemed like all time.

Lunging suddenly up, my fingernails plowed red
rows into his freshly shaved face. "You killed him!" my
voice screamed. "You killed him—Ohhhhh!"

My neck was caught in the *V* of his arm, and I
wanted nothing so much as to breathe again. Releasing
his hold, Pierce wiped the blood from his cheeks. The
air that I greedily sucked into my lungs came rushing
out again, carrying with it a single word that I hurled
at him in a spray of spit.

"Murderer!"

17

As I LAY across my bed I pinched my forearm until the colors changed from white to pink and finally to a crescent of red. If this is nothing but a bad dream a little pain should scare it away. But I can see him still, his face contorted. Harder, pinch harder! The red crescent turned purple. But Anton's sprawled body was still there bleeding across the city sidewalk.

Pierce stood just outside my door talking on the hall phone. ". . . All right, yes, yes, I'll hold. Mr. Bergen, these calls aren't costing you anything. I've reversed the charges."

"Hurry it up. I've got to call my lawyer."

"I'm doing the best I can, Mr. Bergen. My instructions were to bring the girl into Little Rock. Since you'd rather I bring her into our Memphis bureau, I'm gonna have to get permission for that."

"Do what you can."

". . . Hello, Chief Gilford? John Pierce here. We got a virtual confession out of the girl. She knew he was a prisoner of war, and she sheltered him. McFee is out checking the abandoned rooms above the family garage. . . . All she says is that she did it and did it alone. Listen, Chief, I've run into a snag. The father wants her taken into Memphis, wants a certain Memphis lawyer to handle the case . . . . I don't know if he thought of that. Hold on, let me talk to him." Pierce held the receiver against his chest. "Uh, Mr. Bergen. Our bureau chief, Tom Gilford, says we can question her from the Memphis bureau, but that it would pose a problem you might not be aware of."

"What problem?"

"He says that any charges that might come out of the investigation would be processed through the Arkansas courts and that you would be better advised to have an Arkansas lawyer who knows the local courts."

"And I still want her taken into Memphis!" my father said.

My father walked into my bedroom and slumped into the maple rocker. I heard his young voice quiver, but not from rage. "I don't understand. How could you? A girl who is Jewish. You disgrace me, your own father. And for what? A Nazi. A God damn Nazi!" He brought a white handkerchief out of a back pocket and began blowing his nose.

At another time I might have felt his grief was mine. But now his was his and mine was my own and that was burden enough.

He jumped out of the rocker as though the cushion had suddenly been replaced by hot coals. "Tell me why," he shouted, his voice hollow.

"I can't tell you. You wouldn't understand."

"Tell me!" he screamed, but this time he seemed more vulnerable than violent.

"He was good to me."

My father looked as though I had just finished telling him the world's most incredible lie. "Are you going to tell me or do I have to knock it out of you?"

"I've already told you. He was kind to me."

"And I don't believe you. You let him put his hands on your body, didn't you?" His thin lips contorted into a sneer. "You—you filth!"

"That's a lie! Anton's a good man. A better man than you."

"God damn you!" The paleness left his face. "How

160

dare you compare me to that Nazi! Why you—you're no good. From the day you were born you've brought me nothing but misery."

Ruth rushed into the room, brushing past my father. "You've got no call talking to this child like that." She sat down beside me, giving the bed a bounce. "Mr. Bergen, now I only works here and I ain't 'pose to be telling you nothing, but some things needs saying. Lord knows that's the truth." Her arm spread over me like a great shield. "That man from the government didn't say Patty did bad. All I heard she do is let a tired man sleep where nobody else wanted to sleep and gave him food that came from nobody's mouth."

"And I want you to stop interfering in something that's none of your business."

The earth-colored yolks of Ruth's eyes rose to their highest point, leaving a splash of whitness below. "This here is the Lord's business, Mr. Bergen, and I'm trying to do the work He set out for me." Her hands were clasped and her eyes stayed heavenward. After a moment she nodded as though she understood her silent instructions. "God is our refuge and strength, and a help in troubles. Therefore will we not fear, though the earth be removed and the mountains be carried into the midst of the sea. . . . Be still, and know that I am God."

"Ruth, get yourself out of here."

"Listen to the Lord speakin' to you, Mr. Bergen."

Couldn't Ruth see she was wasting her time? "Leave him alone. He doesn't understand," I whispered.

"God almighty is crying out to you to bring forth your humanity. He wants you to quit your tormenting and put your faith in Him."

My father threw Ruth a look that could have split rock. "And now I'm telling you, you've pushed me past my endurance. I think a lot of Patty's meanness is your doing. This family doesn't need you anymore." He took

161

out his wallet and threw a five-dollar bill and three ones onto the bed. One of the singles rested for a moment at the side of the bed before fluttering to the floor. Neither Ruth nor my father made any effort to pick it up. "Now, I'm paying you for the week, but I don't want you here one second longer. Get your things and get out. Now!"

"Lord knows I needs this job, Mr. Bergen. Lord knows I needs the money, but—" Ruth's arm tightened around me. "This child needs me even more than I needs the work. Truth is she does."

"Don't send Ruth away! Please, don't do it." My arms couldn't complete the circle around her waist. "If you never in your life do another thing for me, don't send her away. She's all I have left."

"Take the money, Ruth," said my father in a voice marked by sudden calmness. "And then you tell those fat legs of yours to take you out of here."

18

PIERCE WALKED to the door of my room without entering. "All settled, Mr. Bergen. We're taking the girl into Memphis." Then he gave me a nod. "Better pack a few things."

"How long will she be gone?"

"Don't know, sir. She'd better take a few changes."

I got the smallest of the three suitcases out of the closet and began putting in some clothes like a robot who feels nothing. I wasn't even conscious anymore of wanting anything except maybe to be left alone, and I wasn't even strong on that. Living was too big a deal and dying too much trouble.

When I snapped the case closed the agent asked, "Ready to go?"

"Yes."

My father was shouting into the phone, ". . . Well, get Mr. Kishner out of conference. This is an emergency. Let the Hardwood Dealers of America wait! . . . . No, it's not about my business. I guess I oughta know what kind of a lawyer I need. . . . Less than an hour? Have Mr. Kishner call me back collect at number two five five, Jenkinsville, Arkansas. Got that? Number two five five."

"We're ready, Mr. Bergen," said Pierce.

"I can't leave. I want to be here when the lawyer calls."

"No problem. It's only a couple of blocks to our car. McFee, get the suitcase, will you?"

As I walked past my father I said, "Good-bye," but maybe he didn't hear. At any rate he didn't answer.

The sidewalk was too narrow for three, so Pierce and McFee walked a few steps behind me. Across the street Freddy Dowd looked up from his worm diggings. "Where you going? Someplace?"

"Memphis."

"Boy, oh, boy," he said, letting out his widest grin, "I sure wish I was you!"

I laughed inside. "There are better wishes to wish for, Freddy."

As we came close to my father's store I saw people milling in front. Too many people for a weekday unless today is dollar day. Suddenly, the FBI men were walking at my side. "Stay close to me," whispered Pierce. There were ten, more than that, at least fifteen people and all with fixed faces. They know about me. How could they have found out so soon? Then I spotted Jenkinsville's leading gossip merchant, Mary Wren, holding onto the arm of Reverend Benn's wife.

The agents maneuvered me away from the sidewalk and into the center of Main Street. The crowd followed. A glob of liquid hit me in the back of the neck and when I saw what my hand had wiped away I gagged.

Suddenly a woman's voice called, "Nazi! Nazi!" Other voices joined in. A man's voice, one that I had heard before, shouted, "Jew Nazi—Jew Nazi—Jew Nazi!"

When we reached the car, the mob blocked the doors. "You people are obstructing justice," said Pierce. "Please move back."

"Jew Nazi-lover!" screamed the minister's wife.

Tires screeched to a stop. A car door opened and

164

Sheriff Cauldwell shouted, "Get away from that car. What's the matter with you folks, anyway?"

People slowly moved away from the car, crowding into a huddle on the sidewalk. Sheriff Cauldwell opened the back door of the car for me, and then, whipping out a small black Bible from his shirt pocket, he pressed it into my hand. "Times when I was down this helped lift me up. God bless you."

"Thanks," I said, feeling the tears stinging at my eyes.

McFee drove in second gear all the way down Main Street before taking a right turn onto Highway 64. As we passed McDonald's dairy, I looked down the long dirt road leading to the prison camp. But I knew I wasn't going to find him there or any other place on God's earth.

I was already awake when the phone first rang downstairs at a quarter to eight. By nine there had already been three or four incoming calls. I wondered if they concerned me.

At nine thirty I knew I couldn't put it off any longer. I would go downstairs and face my grandparents. Last night it was pretty late when the agents brought me here, and Grandmother Fried said that I looked very tired and she took me straight to bed. This morning, though, it might be different. She might get around now to the questions she hadn't asked.

I saw her at the kitchen table, stirring a cup of coffee with one hand and holding the phone with the other. "You sure about Harry selling the store? Things blow over. People forget. . . . Pearl, I'll talk to Poppa. . . . Didn't I say I would? If Harry had been maybe a little nice to us all these years then I know Poppa would say, sure. Now, I don't know. . . ." My grandmother looked up as I entered the kitchen. "Pearl, I have to go now. Patty just woke up. . . . Yes, Pearl, I'll talk. I'll talk! Tonight, after supper. Good-bye."

"My father has to sell the store?"

"Maybe he does, maybe he doesn't. Who knows? My daughter always makes a *gontzeh tsimmes* out of everything."

"And my father wants to go to work for Grandfather?"

"Your mother wants it; only *Gott in Himmel* knows what your daddy wants."

Grandmother brought me a perfectly oval omelet. "I'm sorry to cause you all this trouble," I said.

"Trouble? An omelet is trouble?"

"Well, that and having to stay up to let me in last night."

"It's nice having you—" she said, patting my cheek—"even if it's because of this *mish-mosh*."

"*Mish-mosh?*"

"What else? Does a person have to ask for credentials before they can give food to a hungry man? Are you responsible because you gave nourishment to a bad man? The whole business is a *mishegoss*."

"I'm glad you're not angry with me."

"What is there to be angry about? I have messages for you. I'm going to drive you to Lawyer Kishner's office at quarter till eleven, and he's going to take you himself to the FBI. Also a friend called." She began searching through a pad of paper. "I wrote it down myself. Here! It's a Miss Charlene Madlee. She's coming by tonight to see you."

Mostly, I told the FBI everything they wanted to know, and I told it about a dozen times to four different agents. One question they seemed keen on asking was if anybody else knew. Sometimes they'd just ask, "Who else knew?" or "Why are you taking all the blame?" Things like that. But always I gave the same answer— "Nobody else knew. It was only me."

It was after four in the afternoon when the boss agent, Mr. Wilhelm, told one of the younger agents to drive me back to my grandmother's. "I don't believe we'll be needing you anymore, Patty, but you'd better stay here in Memphis for a while. Things are unsettled in Jenkinsville."

"Unsettled?"

"Well, I understand your parents are being harassed."

"How?"

"Telephone calls, a store window broken, things like that."

"Why would they bother them? Can't you tell people that they had nothing to do with it? They didn't even know."

Mr. Wilhelm scratched his forehead like he was trying to come up with an answer for me. "When people's emotions are involved they don't want to listen."

At eight o'clock my grandmother opened the door for Charlene as I stood at the top of the stairs, waiting for my trembling to subside. Would she hate me?

"It was kind of you to let me come tonight, Mrs. Fried." If there was any hate in Charlene's voice I couldn't catch it.

"Our pleasure, Miss—"

"Madlee. Charlene Madlee."

"Yes, well, Miss Madlee, Patty needs all her friends now. You saw the evening paper?"

"Oh, yes, I read them as well as write for them."

"You write? For newspapers? You told me you were a friend of Patty's. Friends we need; reporters we don't."

"Believe me, Mrs. Fried, I am a friend. When we met during the summer, Patty told me that her grandparents lived in Hein Park. Also I came here tonight to bring you encouraging news."

As I walked down the stairs, Charlene gave me a real smile. Still my friend. My grandfather pulled out

167

a dining room chair for Charlene. "My wife makes the best strudel in the world. Wait'll you taste!" He smacked his lips.

Charlene ate a forkful. "You know, Mrs. Fried, I think your husband is right. You do make the world's best strudel."

"It's wonderful," I said. "I remember reading somewhere that kissing doesn't last, but cookery does."

My grandfather jumped up from the host's chair to give Grandmother a noisy kiss on her cheek. "Does that answer your question, young lady?"

"Sam!"

We all laughed, then abruptly turned to Charlene as if hoping she might give us something of substance to laugh about.

"I talked today to Charles Hammett," said Charlene.

"He's the editor of the *Commercial Appeal?*" asked Grandfather.

"He's our publisher. Well, Mr. Hammett had lunch with a high official from the Justice Department, which would be the agency responsible for initiating legal actions in such cases as Patty's. The feeling is that the government would be very reluctant to prosecute a twelve-year-old under the Treason Act. Also he mentioned that our allies would consider us barbaric if we did such a thing."

Grandfather clapped his hands. "Thank God! I knew this American government was 100 per cent O.K. After all, what did my granddaughter do that's so terrible? She's only twelve, so she didn't act wisely, O.K. But she meant good, you have to admit that. And do you think for one minute that fellow, *aleva-sholem,* told Patty that he was an escaped prisoner? Also one other point, excuse me for bringing this up, Miss Madlee. I recognize that you aren't of our faith, but do you think that if we were Protestants there would be all this hullabaloo?"

"I'm certain there wouldn't, Mr. Fried. There's no question that this gave some people an excuse to parade their anti-Semitism. But all the interest isn't anti-Semitic. Some people may find love and brotherhood in the story. The Memphis bureau of United Press sent it over the international wires, which means that tonight people throughout the world will be reading about how a Jewish girl befriended a German boy."

"I pray to God," said Grandmother, "that when they read about Patty they'll feel a little closer to their brothers no matter what faith or nationality."

"I'm just glad it's over," said Grandfather.

Charlene looked confused. "I'm sorry if I implied that all charges against Patty will be dropped; I meant only the serious charges of treason. The man from the Justice Department felt that if there was a public outcry the state of Arkansas might wish to prosecute Patty on a lesser charge."

"But I'm not guilty of a lesser charge! They can call it treason, but they can't call it anything else."

"At best, Patty, all charges will be dropped," said Charlene. "But if the Arkansas politicians are pushed to move against you they could easily get you on, say, a delinquency charge. In that way the Federal Government is off the hook, and people will still feel that justice has been served."

Grandmother clasped her hand to her heart. "You don't think—it's not possible that they would send my granddaughter to jail?"

"It's only the slightest of possibilities," said Charlene slowly, as though she were choosing her words with inordinate care. "But there does still exist the chance that Patty might be sent to reform school."

19

O! Little town of Bethlehem,
How still we see thee lie!
Above thy deep and dreamless sleep,
The silent stars go——

The music from the car radio turned to static. "Too far from Jonesboro to get much reception," said Mr. Calvin Grimes.

"Guess so."

"Well," he said, snapping the radio off, "reckon that's it."

"Yes, sir, guess it is," I answered, trying to keep up my end of the conversation.

The sky was purply, deepening even as I watched, warning of the approach of darkness and maybe even of snow. Along the highway rows of never-been-painted tenant shacks glowed with the softness of kerosene lamps. Their windows without curtains gave quick exposures of tenant families, mostly colored, sitting around the supper table.

Then with sudden speed Mr. Grimes swerved from the right- to the left-hand lane to pass a poky tractor. "Feller should know enough," he said, "to have his lights on this time of day, wouldn't you think? Slow-moving vehicle like that."

"Yes, sir, he sure should," I said.

As the road turned off to the left, there was a definite rise from the flatness of the delta lands. Beginning in me was a matching feeling of ascent. Where have you been for such a long time, Hope? Remember the last time you came paying me a visit? Wait six years, you told me, only six years and I would have outside beauty—more even than my mother's—while inside I would grow beautiful like Ruth. And then I would find Anton again, and he would love me for everything I was, everything I had become.

Suddenly a chuckle started up in me and then a second and a third. Without moving my eyes from the side window I could tell Mr. Grimes had turned to look at me. "Girl, if you've got yourself a funny, why don't you share it?"

"Uh, no, sir, I don't actually know any jokes or anything like that, it was just that—Well, I was thinking of a friend of mine whom I liked being with so much because he could always make things fun. Know what I mean?"

"Reckon I do." Mr. Grimes measured out his words. "Them kind of folks always nice to have around."

"Not just big things," I explained because for some reason I really wanted him to understand, "but little things too. Things that lotsa folks wouldn't even find amusing."

"Girl, that's one of the Lord's blessings. Laughter and them that makes it. Like he gives it to some folks to be strong, others to be rich. Now, to me he gave a fine wife and four good boys. Them's blessings, girl. Everybody got to find the Lord's bounty and give thanks. You know your blessings? Counted them? Laid them aside and said your thanks?"

I thought of Ruth, Grandmother, and Grandfather. I thought of the frizzle that had finally grown out of my hair. And then I thought of him, and I wondered if a blessing is still a blessing if it lasts for only a little while?

Then with my eyes quite open Anton's face came through. I closed my eyes to blot out all possible distractions. He was smiling that smile, I'd seen it before when he said to me, "Remember, P.B., remember when . . ." But I didn't hear the rest of his words. I was just too filled up with feelings of pleasure and privilege to think that in those short days together we had begun making memories.

"Ya gettin' hungry?" Mr. Grimes' dry voice popped my bubble of reverie. "There's a restaurant down the road jest past Lambert. We could stop there for hamburgers 'cause I'm not in a million years gonna make Bolton till after ten o'clock. I jest don't know whether one of them matrons would save you a bite of supper. Wouldn't bet my last nickel on it, tell you that fer sure."

In the distance a large red neon sign blinked:

SHANLEY'S GULF STATION
Good Food—Good Gas

Even a car-length away from Shanley's front door the smell of things fried—hamburgers, potatoes, and onions—was pretty powerful.

At the back of the restaurant a fancy jukebox changed from red to purple to blue as it blared forth, "Shuffle on down to Memphis Town. . . . Oh, shuffle on down to Memphis Town. Ain't got no money but I'll show you around."

I followed Mr. Grimes to the only empty booth, empty of people but not of their dishes. Ashes and cigarette butts filled the glass ash tray to capacity.

Our waitress, who was about sixteen and I guess you'd call her pretty, wore beaded Indian moccasins

172

but no stockings over her hairy legs. She dropped a menu wrapped in a cellophane folder on the table and left without bothering to clean up the mess. With the back of his arm Mr. Grimes swept the dirty dishes to the edge of the table. "I like it clean and neat when I eat," he said. "Seems like ever since the war, waitresses been going from bad to worse."

As he shook his head, I noticed deep lines which ran like chicken wire from the corners of his eyes clean out to his hairline. Mr. Grimes was far away from being young and, judging from the leanness of his body, he'd never been especially strong.

After we had eaten our hamburgers and french fries and drunk down our coffee, Mr. Grimes waved to the waitress. "What kinda pie you got?"

She gave her hair, which was the color of brown wrapping paper, a good scratching. "We're all out of apple." Nodding in the direction of the counter, she said, "Gave that feller the last piece."

"What kind have you got left?" asked Mr. Grimes, not bothering to keep the irritation out of his voice.

" 'Bout the only thing I know we got is some sugar doughnuts left over from the morning and some lemon meringue pie."

"I'll take a piece of that meringue," he said, and he looked over at me. "Ya wanna piece too?"

Behind the counter a penciled sign read: All Pies 12¢. "Well, uh, no, thank you. I guess I don't care for any pie today."

"Better get some," encouraged Mr. Grimes. "This might be your last decent meal for a while."

When I laid my fork down the pie plate had only a few pin-point-sized crumbs left on it. I wanted to send my fork after those too, but didn't want Mr. Grimes to think I was still a little hungry. I felt his eyes upon me and looked up.

"Oh, by the way," he said, "I don't think you

oughta go mentioning to anybody that we stopped off for a bite of supper 'cause jest strictly speakin', I ain't 'spose to stop nowhere with no prisoner."

Prisoner? Me? The judge never once used that word: "I hereby sentence Patricia Ann Bergen to be committed to the Arkansas Reformatory for Girls at Bolton, Arkansas, for a period of not more than six months nor less than four months." But if Mr. Grimes calls me a prisoner, I guess he ought to know. Funny, the word has no sting. But then nothing has much sting anymore.

He rubbed his fist back and forth across his chin. "So we'll jest keep this between you and me, O.K.?"

I didn't want him fearing for his job on my account. "Mr. Grimes, it was sure nice of you to stop so I could have something to eat, and I will never say anything to anybody. If I got you in trouble—Pow! God should strike me down dead."

His smile showed a vacancy between two front teeth. "Lord, girl, I sure don't want nothing like that happening to you."

I felt myself smiling back. He was really quite nice. "The whole thing is, and I thought about it quite a lot, it's not true what they said about me. In court they called me a person of no loyalties—a traitor. But it just couldn't be true 'cause it was my loyalties that got me into trouble in the first place, know what I mean?"

He nodded. "I read about it in the papers, how you helped out that German boy."

I was grateful he called him a boy; better than the others calling him Nazi or spy. "I wanted to help him because he wasn't a Nazi or a spy, and he wasn't even mean. Anton was the kindest, smartest man I've ever known. I wanted to tell that to the judge so he'd understand why I had to hide him. Why I had to help him stay free. But Mr. Kishner just kept shaking his head No."

174

Mr. Grimes was looking at me as though Anton couldn't be all those things I said he was. Why did I have to go spouting off to him? What made me think he would understand when nobody else could? "Don't you think," I asked, hearing the anger in my voice, "that a German can be good?"

"Oh, I reckon on St. Peter opening up them pearly gates for some Germans," he said. "Now, there ain't no need to go getting your dander up jest 'cause I don't understand who's this Mr. Kishner."

"I'm sorry. He's the man, the lawyer, my father hired to tell my side of the story in court. Only thing is he kept saying that the really important things were not pertinent to the case."

"Them lawyers are tricky fellers all right," said Mr. Grimes. "One time, oh, this was two or three years ago, I was taking a feller name of Cranston Hollis to the Cummins Prison Farm."

He waved his empty coffee cup in the air and Miss Beaded Moccasins filled both of our cups from a steaming pot. "Well, Mr. Cranston Hollis, he was one big man. President of a state savings bank in North Little Rock. Only thing was when the bank examiner came to look at the ledger he found that Mr. Hollis' bank was shy one hundred and eighty-five thousand dollars and that ain't even counting the change."

I said, "That's a lot."

"Ooh-whee, I'll say it is. More money than I'll make in all my working lifetime. Well, this Mr. Hollis, he was one smart man, told me eight people other than him worked in that bank. Six of them had more opportunity than he did to take the money. But his lawyer didn't even entertain the notion that he was defending an innocent man. So Mr. Hollis' advice to anyone who has to go up before the bar of justice is to beware of at least two people: the lawyer the state hires to convict you and the lawyer you hire to defend yourself."

It was easier for me to agree with poor Mr. Cranston Hollis now than before my experience with Mr. Kishner. But it wasn't exactly his fault. I mean, actually he didn't want to take my case in the first place. My father had especially wanted Mr. Kishner because he was known as a really big Memphis lawyer, and I know for a fact how proud the Beth Zion Synagogue is that he is one of them.

When my father first phoned him, Mr. Kishner said that it wasn't the kind of thing he wanted to get involved in, and besides since the case would be tried in the Arkansas courts, it would be much better to hire a local, non-Jewish attorney. Somebody who knew all the local judges and wouldn't be afraid to speak out.

After Mr. Kishner refused to take my case, my father placed another long distance call to Memphis. This time it was to Morris Frank, president of Beth Zion, who I think my father had met before. Mr. Frank said that he had known Harold Kishner for more than thirty years and if anybody could get him to take the case he could. And he did.

On the very next day Mr. Kishner's thin and unsmiling secretary led me into an office of dark wood, real leather chairs, and an oriental rug of such fire and density that it must have taken a hundred weavers all their lifetimes to complete. A window behind the great man gave a fine view of the Memphis skyline.

The lawyer sighed into the receiver, "Leo, why can't you keep in mind that we're treating it as a tax preference item?"

When he finally placed the receiver on the hook he nodded at me without smiling. I nodded back while forcing a smile. He got up from his chair. I edged forward in mine. Finally he said he was my lawyer, hired to be, and that he was going to see if he could help me.

He asked me to tell my story just as it happened, and as I did he scribbled notes on a long yellow pad. Every so often he would interrupt to ask a question or clarify a point. A couple of times and in slightly different ways he asked if I were afraid of Anton, afraid that harm might come to either me or my family if I failed to obey.

Mr. Kishner's lips thinned when I shook my head. "I was never afraid."

Then he tried to get me to say I was too young to understand that Anton was an escaped prisoner. How could I not have understood that? I wanted to tell him that I had some pride left and that they could accuse me of being a traitor, but not of being stupid. But I kept quiet.

Finally Mr. Kishner replaced his fountain pen in his onyx desk set and rose, looking me over closely for the first time, and I knew that he would speak. "Young lady, you have embarrassed Jews everywhere. Because your loyalty is questionable, then every Jew's loyalty is in question." He sighed before adding, "I just wanted you to know."

Outside Shanley's Restaurant the air came up sharp and clean. "Cold enough for you?" asked Mr. Grimes.

"Oh, I don't mind," I said. A vision of snow on distant mountaintops came to me and I was close to asking if there were mountains at Bolton, but fear that he would say there was only flat land kept the question unasked. With the end of Anton, hope had taken to its sickbed, if not its deathbed.

I found a small bit of courage within, not enough for mountains, but maybe for a little snow. I decided to squander it. "Any chance we might get snow for Christmas?"

Mr. Grimes looked to the right and then the left, shifted into second, and entered the two-lane highway before speaking. "Weatherman on the radio said the Carolinas might get some, but I ain't never heard of snow taking no geography lessons. Back in '38 or '39—

'38 it was—we got almost an inch of snow for Christmas."

"I'd like that to happen again," I said as I brought my shoeless feet up beside me on the car seat. My head found a resting place in the bough of my arm. I felt myself going down, down to sleep.

Against my arm, tapping. "Wake up, girl. We're almost there."

"Wha—" I stifled my yawn inside the crook of my elbow.

"We're coming into Bolton, thought you'd like to see it. The school's east of town."

"Oh," I said, conscious of feeling nothing but sleepy.

Then, spanning the width of the street, strings of Christmas lights—red and blue, green and yellow. A lighted movie marquee announced, *The Five Sullivans* and Xmas cartoons.

"I saw that movie!" I said, coming alive. "All about five brothers, sailors on this ship that was sunk. Saddest thing I've ever seen. Try to see that movie if you get the chance."

"Nope," answered Mr. Grimes. "Don't have to spend my money for sadness. Plenty of that to be had for free."

Mr. Grimes followed the road through town, past two blocks of houses, a gas station, and then open land. Headlights picked up a black iron fence, and as the car swung through open gates I saw a sign with the Arkansas state seal. It read:

THE JASPER E. CONRAD
ARKANSAS REFORMATORY FOR GIRLS
BOLTON, ARKANSAS

The lights were on in the three-story building. In the darkness it looked no different from any other three-story brick. No! There was something different. The windows were covered, all covered, with diamond-shaped, heavy wire screening. At the Memphis Zoo they use the same kind of screening for the animals.

20

My eyes opened. I measured the bleakness of the morning against the painted grayness of the walls and estimated the time to be six thirty. Ever since I had been here, and today marked the thirty-second morning, there had been this new ability of mine to awaken, fully awake, without stretching or yawning. Part of it was knowing that this thirty minutes before the wake-up bell was the only time that belonged to me.

All right, get to it, I told myself. This is finally going to be the morning when things come to me: My plans for a lifetime. I gave myself the usual instructions: Try new roads; check out all byways, explore every possibility. But my mind hadn't even finished its pep talk when the familiar vision intruded. "Go away," I said out loud, "I have to be practical." I couldn't risk everything on such a slim hope. It didn't make sense!

Think practical; think about living in Memphis with Grandmother and Grandfather. My father wouldn't hear of it. Didn't he tell the FBI that they had no right to take me to Grandma's that evening after they had finished questioning me?

Then think about going away to school, to some private place in New England where nobody would know me. My mother wouldn't let me. Even before the scandal I clipped an ad from the back pages of

The Ladies' Home Journal showing a girl about my age smiling at her horse, and underneath the picture it read, "Briar Cliff: an experience in living."

My mother only glanced at the ad before starting to laugh, "Where do you dream up such ideas?" she demanded. "Are you such a fancy girl you need such a fancy school?" No possibility there, none at all.

Well, I've heard about people working their way through school, and there are things I can do. I could take care of the horses. I'd love that, but even if that job were filled there are other things. Cooks need helpers, or maybe I could use the work experience that I'm getting here. As I brought my hands from beneath the blanket bleach attacked my nostrils. That smell may have been part of my imagination, but my red, chapped hands weren't. No, I don't want to work in anybody's laundry anywhere, anymore.

The vision was still there waiting for me, soft and appealing. I let it in. It's six years from now. I'm eighteen. The war is over. With my thousand-dollar war bond, I have money enough to take a train to New York and from there a ship to Germany. Another train ride and I'm in Göttingen. At the train station I change into my prettiest dress before dialing the number. No, not at the station, better at a hotel.

A woman answers and I ask, "Mrs. Reiker?"

"This is Mrs. Reiker," says the voice in elegant English.

"Mrs. Reiker," I say slowly, "I'm an American. My name is Patricia Bergen. I knew your son, Anton." There is only silence, so I stumble on. "We were friends back when he was a prisoner of war, in America."

"You knew Anton?" she asks, her voice hollow like it was traveling over great distance, or great sorrow.

I breathe in deeply before answering. "Yes, I knew Anton. We were friends. I tried to help him."

"You tried to help him? Where are you?" asks Mrs. Reiker, sounding suddenly energized.

I tell her that I'm right here in Göttingen and she asks, "Could you possibly have dinner with us tonight? And of course any traveling companions you have would be most welcome."

"Well, I don't actually have any traveling companions," I say.

"Then you must stay with us," she replies. "We have a large house. We could make you most comfortable."

My heart floated up like a helium ballon until the ringing of the wake-up bell punctured it. I cried out against the intrusion, wondering if there weren't some way to hold onto the vision. It seemed unfair. I had lost my chance to become a member of the family.

"Hey, Natz, you gonna get up? Scrambled egg day."

I pulled the covers down to look directly into the Raggedy Ann eyes of my roommate, Mavis McCall. "I'm getting up," I said, wiggling my feet to give the impression of forward movement. "Could you please stop calling me Natz?"

"Geez, whatta ya want me to call ya, Nazi or Spy like them others do?" Mavis managed to look as though I had just spit upon her grandmother's grave.

"Well, if it's all the same to you, you could call me Patty or even the name I was born with, Patricia." Mavis looked a long way from being convinced so I added, "I don't call you Thief, do I?"

In the cafeteria line Mavis stood in front of me as rigidly silent as the angel on the topmost point of the room's Christmas tree. "Don't they know that Christmas trees are supposed to be taken down as soon as Christmas is over?" I asked.

"Can't go 'bout taking a Christmas tree down on a Sunday!" she said, sounding shocked at my ignorance. "Wouldn't be right."

I was grateful that she was still talking to me. "No, guess not," I answered.

As Mavis wiped the last crumbs from her plate with a piece of white bread, I saw her eyes check my plate. "I haven't touched my eggs," I said, pushing my plate towards her and wondering why the eggs didn't taste as powdery to her as they did to me.

Mavis scraped them onto her plate, then paused with her fork directly over my mound of grits. Her eyes sought my permission. "I'm all finished eating," I said.

"You ain't much of an eater, is you?" she said and then added in lieu of thanks, "Patty."

After breakfast the day room, with its hard-backed chairs lined like soldiers against the wall, was empty. The girls had all gone over to the nondenominational services in the chapel. On my first Sunday here I had gone because the head matron, Miss Laud (secretly called "Miss Bald" due to the fact that pink skin was beginning to show through her hair) kept emphasizing that the services were absolutely nondenominational. Now maybe, and I'll give her the benefit of the doubt, the services are nondenominational for Baptists, Methodists, and Jehovah's Witnesses, but they are definitely not nondenominational for a Jewish girl. I say this because the minister spent just about his whole sermon talking about the method the Jews used when they killed Jesus.

The clock high above the doorway of the day room read ten till ten, yet the grayness of the morning hung on. On the side table sat the room's most valuable item, a mahogany radio with an arched top. Usually it was ablare with sad-sounding cowboys singing of girls they had loved and lost, but for the time being it sat quietly neglected.

I snapped the knob to the right and waited for the tubes to warm. I tried to find something good to listen to on a Sunday morning. Phil Baker and his *Sixty-four Dollar Question* wasn't till evening and so was *Baby Snooks*. Even Andre Kostelanetz and his orchestra wasn't till later.

"For God so loved the world, that he gave his only begotten Son, that—"

I moved the dial. This time to singing. "Where he leads me, I shall follow—"

And another turn of the dial. "Tell me why it is, dear friends," cried out a man's voice in apparent anguish, "that people will believe the promise of a bank. Give us your money, we'll keep it safe. And they'll believe the promise of a boss. Work for me, and I'll give you money. Then why is it that these same people have trouble believing in the greatest promise ever given to mankind? Jesus made that promise to you, and he made it to me. And this was his promise: Whosoever believeth in me shall be given life everlasting."

I snapped the knob to the left, and, except for the steady hissing of the radiator, the room was silent.

Back in my room the thick Sunday edition of the *Memphis Commercial Appeal,* a gift subscription from Charlene Madlee, lay on my bed. It was nice having a lady like that for a friend. And I liked having my very own newspaper subscription. I mean besides reading it, it was nice in another way too. It was the something good (instead of always the something bad) that set me apart. I wasn't like them, like the others, and the paper was proof of that.

After my trial Charlene Madlee was the only reporter (and the courtroom was filled with them) who came over to say she was sorry. And she was too! I caught a look on her face of genuine distress. On my second day at Bolton I received her first note. I read it so many times that it became engraved on my brain.

Patty,
I'm sending you a subscription to my paper
with the hope that you will enjoy reading it.
Keep smiling!

Charlene Madlee

And in each reading of Charlene's note I scoured her words for the gift of friendship. Sometimes, like an optical illusion, I found it, and other times I didn't.

Anyway I wrote Charlene back, thanking her and saying the thing I liked most to read were the stories that carried her by-line. That wasn't hard to say. People like honest compliments, I know that. It was what I said next that made me hesitate because it sounded presumptuous. "I still think I'd like to study to become some kind of reporter or writer someday." But she didn't think I was just a presumptuous kid, because she wrote me right back, a whole page.

Footsteps. Determined footsteps came echoing down the corridor. Miss Laud? What would she want me for? I'm not breaking any rules: no cigarettes, no shoes on the bed, door open. About the nondenominational services? But I've already explained that, how the services go against my beliefs. I won't go!

As the footsteps stopped at my door, fear took hold. I forced myself to look up at the full standing authority of Miss Evelyn Laud.

"You know a Nigra named Ruth Hughes?"

"Ma'am?"

"A Nigra named Ruth Hughes, says she's your nanny, that right?"

"Uh, yes, ma'am, that's right."

Miss Laud nodded.

"Well, go on down to the visitors' room and see her."

"Ma'am?" I asked, like one who has suddenly stopped understanding the English language.

"Well, go down and see her," repeated Miss Laud in tones loud enough for the deaf.

Through the open archway of the visitors' room I could see Ruth, her back towards me, looking out the mesh-covered window to the courtyard below. She was wearing a dress I had never seen before, deep blue like the sky gets toward evening. It looked to be crepe and good enough not only for Sunday but for Easter Sunday as well. Strange, she didn't seem to hear my approach for her gaze never strayed from the window.

"Ruth?"

Like a spring suddenly released, she turned, her brown face showing a wide, welcoming smile. But it wasn't the smile that caught me quite as much as her eyes. They had this shine, a gloss that I remembered seeing once before, but I couldn't quite remember when.

Arms circled me, bringing me close. "Patty, Honey Babe, how you doing?" A fragrance of bath powder scented gardenia. "You doin' all right, Honey?" My head found its resting place next to her shoulder and I closed my eyes while I silently prayed for the world to go away. "Are they treating you all right here?"

I nodded my head Yes, but I didn't know for sure whether she got my message, so I said, "I guess they are. Yes." And there in the protection of her circle, I felt freshly born.

Ruth, still with an arm around my waist, led me to a wooden bench next to the radiator, but before we sat down she pushed me an arm's length away and gave me a careful looking over. "You shore ain't doin' no overeating hereabouts, are you?"

"On Sundays we have scrambled eggs for breakfast," I said, wondering if my answer fit the question.

"There's six other days need accounting for."

"Well, mostly they serve grits for breakfast."

Ruth looked angry. "You never would eat no grits."

"I eat them sometimes," I said, feeling that we should somehow be spending this time together on better things. "Tell me something. What's new in Jenkinsville?"

"Same old town it's always been, Honey. When

186

the Bible says that there ain't nothing new under the sun, I think they musta had Jenkinsville in mind," Ruth laughed, enjoying her own joke. When her face resettled she added, "Tell you this, I got myself a new job, keeps house for the colored schoolteacher, Miz Cora Mae Ford. You knows her?"

I said that I did while the feeling of betrayal swept over me.

Ruth went on. "She and her husband, Robert, he's got himself a good job too, drives one of them trucks for Dixie Transport. Well, they got themselves three of the cutest children. Now the baby, Michael Augustus, ain't even walking yet and I declare if he ain't 'bout the sweetest little thing I ever did see."

I told myself to forget it. Ruth didn't just up and desert me, remember that. She was fired. Fired! She has to make a living, get along as best as she can. And if she didn't care for me, would she have made this long trip just to see me?

"How did you ever manage to get here, Ruth?"

Her eyes grew wide and the gloss disappeared. It must have had something to do with how the light from the window struck her eyes. "Would you ever think that your old Ruth would come a-visiting in a big vehicle driven by a chauffeur?"

"Really? You're kidding me?"

She put a look of mock disgust on her face. "Well, if'n a Greyhound Bus ain't a big vehicle and if'n a uniformed driver ain't a chauffeur then I don't know much of nothing no more."

I felt the muscles about my mouth tugging upward into an unnatural or, at least, seldom-used position. "I'm really glad you came to see me. Must have been a long trip."

"No-o-o-o," said Ruth. "Wasn't too long 'cause I got to see me places I ain't never seed before. Heard about, but never seed. Places like Wynne City, Jonesboro, Bolton, places like that." She suddenly jumped up and rushed across the room to a red-and-white-striped shopping bag.

Reaching low into the bag, she brought out a box whose lettering was clearly readable through the white tissue paper wrappings. "Ginger snaps. Thanks. You know they're my very favorites." I gave Ruth a quick hug. "I'm sorry I don't have anything for you this year, but I didn't get to do any Christmas shopping."

"Now that don't make no nevermind, Patty Babe, 'cause come next Christmas I'm gonna give you a list more'n six feet long. But right now I got you a little somethin' else." She reached into her shopping bag to bring out a yellow shoe box tied with red paper ribbon. I broke the string to find a whole family of fried chicken breasts, each one sitting on its very own pink paper napkin.

"Nothing there but the breasts," she said. "See, Ruth remembers."

And I saw too that Ruth had remembered her own rule about the proper frying of chicken. "Secret is," she used to say, "to fry it, and fry it done in corn meal." And while the chicken fried, there was something else she always did. She'd break an egg or two into a bowl of corn meal, throw in a chopped-up onion, and then she'd drop spoonfuls of the batter into the pan next to the chicken. Hush puppies. I don't think I ever in my life had fried chicken without them.

I pinched off a crispy piece of skin and placed it on my tongue. "Haven't had anything this good since I've been here."

"Miz Bergen, she been up visiting you?"

Ruth's question sounded vaguely disloyal, maybe because any true answer would be pointedly disloyal. "She's got a bad back. Says long trips make it worse. Have you seen her? Any of them?"

Her face brightened. "In the Sav-Mor Market a

couple of Fridays ago I heard this little voice a-calling, 'Ruth! Ruth!' and when I turns around sweet little Sharon comes a-rushing to my arms. 'Ruth,' she says to me, 'where you been so long?' " She shook her head like she was still short an answer. "Poor little thing, and her all the time asking, 'Where you been so long?' "

"You saw my mother too?"

"I surely did. She was nice to me too, said she was glad to see I was gettin' on all right. I 'members more'n fifteen years ago when your folks moved to Jenkinsville to open the store. Folks, white and colored, said Miz Bergen was the best lookin' woman to ever come to town, and I reckon she still is."

"She say anything, Ruth? I mean, did she mention me at all?"

Ruth looked surprised. "Why, shore she did, Honey. You her daughter, ain't you?"

"What did she say?"

"Why, she said 'bout what any mother would say."

I waited to see if Ruth was going to add anything more 'cause vagueness wasn't exactly her natural state. I watched while she looked down and began adjusting the gold band on her left hand.

"Ruth, I would very much appreciate your telling me the truth. The whole truth. Please!"

"Patty, Honey, I ain't never lied to you and I ain't gonna start lying now, but the truth be known, Miz Bergen didn't say too much. But I'll tell you everything I recollect. Well, let's see now," she said, warming up. "Told me she gets letters from you and how you always say you're getting along fine."

I nodded Yes.

"And she told me how she had just sent off a sweater to you through the mails."

"It's the one I'm wearing."

Ruth looked at the sweater and I hoped that I hadn't distracted her. Then she gave me a look like she had turned a little shy. "And Miz Bergen said"—Ruth gave her wedding band a full turn—"she said I was the only one knows how to handle you."

Anger blazed within me. "That's all they ever think about—handling me, controlling me! Why can't they just let me be?"

I watched Ruth shake her head like she didn't quite know what to say anymore. But I felt like I just had to ask her the question I was always asking myself.

"Ruth, I want you to tell me something. You know me better than anybody else. What's really wrong with me?"

"Oh, Honey Babe!" Ruth shook her head like she was trying to shake my words from her ears. "There ain't nothing wrong with you—nothing a few years and a few pounds won't take care of."

"There's gotta be!" My voice was high enough for scaling mountains. "There's just gotta be something or I wouldn't always be getting into trouble, having people hate me."

"When you get older you're gonna see that sometimes it looks like most of the good folks done gone and acquired most of the troubles. Yes, siree! Even the Lord Jesus could've 'voided getting himself crucified if he could've learned to stay out of trouble." It sounded as though Ruth was pretty close to blasphemy, and I searched her face for a secret sign made only to God that she was just kidding. She gave me a squeeze. "Sometimes I shore wish you knew how to go pussyfooting around your pa and your ma, but then I says to myself, if Patty learned pussyfooting then it wouldn't hardly be Patty no more."

"Even if you don't know for 100 per cent positive sure," I encouraged, "there must be things that you suspect about me. And if I knew I'd begin working on ridding myself of them. Only first I've got to be sure what's wrong."

"Don't ask me to tell you something I don't know.

There ain't nothing bad about you, and that's the God's truth. I've cared for chillun white and I've cared for chillun black. I've loved every single one of them, but nary a one as much as you, Patty Babe. Nary a single one."

"You couldn't love me as much as you do Sharon."

"Don't you go telling me what I couldn't do! 'Cause I knows what I knows. And from that first day I walked into your house I loved you the most, and I loves you the most today."

"It's so hard to believe."

"Why, I ain't even the only one. He loved you. Anton did. With my own eyes I saw that man come rushing out of his hiding place to save you. And I saw his face, and I ain't never gonna forget what was written there. 'Cause it said: 'I'd give my own life to save her.' "

"Maybe that's true. He gave me his ring so I'd never forget that he loved me, and that I was a person of value. Only thing is I lost the ring, and then gradually I guess I lost its meaning."

Ruth snapped open her pocketbook. "Honey Babe, you didn't lose your ring. I heard you tell that to the man from the FBI and you musta told that story so many times, you come to believe it." She held up the ring. "You gave me this for safekeeping when I told you your pa was coming home to see you. Remember?"

I brought his ring to my lips, barely believing it. "He did love me," I said to Ruth. "And maybe one day my mother and father will too."

Ruth's eyes came level with mine and I could feel her resources rushing forward like front line soldiers to battle. "I ain't nevah 'fore cast me no 'spersions on other folks' folks," she said slowly, "but your folks ain't nevah gonna feel nothing good regarding you. And they ain't the number one best quality folks neither. They shore ain't. When I goes shoppin' and I sees the label stamped, 'Irregular' or 'Seconds,' then I knows

I won't have to pay so much for it. But you've got yourself some irregular seconds folks, and you've been paying more'n top dollar for them. So jest don't go a-wishing for what ain't nevah gonna be."

"But I always thought it was me. Because I was bad."

"You ain't bad!"

I kissed my ring again, and then gave Ruth the strongest squeeze I could manage. "Nothing has changed, but I feel different. Good. Like a good person! And that was what all the whispering was about!"

"What whispering you talkin' bout?"

"Every so often, there's this whispering going on inside me. And whispering's always so soft I could never make it out before."

"Was it God a-speakin' to you?" asked Ruth, her eyes wide.

I never thought about it being God. What would God be wasting his time with a twelve-year-old for? "I don't think," I said, "that God would whisper, do you?"

Ruth pressed her lips together. "The ways of the Lord are filled with wonder and mystery."

"Well, just the same, it didn't sound like God. I think, actually, it was truth. Truth growing inside like a baby, and for a long time it was just too little, too weak to say anything. But day by day it gains strength."

"And to what use is you gonna put this truth?"

"Well, maybe, I don't know right at this moment, but I do know that in spite of everything I did and everything people say about me I don't feel bad, not anymore. I'm not bad, and right now that seems important."

Ruth drew me to her and I could tell that she understood too.

21

TOGETHER WE WATCHED an icy rain make slapping sounds against the window. After a while Ruth said something, something about her galoshes which I didn't quite hear, probably because I had become too deeply encased in comfort. With my eyes closed, feeling the warmth of Ruth against me, I could believe in so many things. Ruth had never been fired; I had never been found out; and Anton had never been killed. He was waiting for me now, alive in the hide-out, and when night came, we'd go away. Morocco or Mexico. Somewhere, anywhere, together.

"And I was halfways out the door when I said to myself, ain't no guarantees about no weather so I went right back and got 'em."

"Good idea," I said. "I'm glad you remembered."

We fell into quiet again, and it was comfortable. Then Ruth began humming and soon she found the words, "Nobody knows the troubles I've seen. Glory hallelujah."

"I don't want to go home again," I said with a suddenness that surprised even me.

"Well, you ain't got nowhere else for going. You's too old for 'dopting and too young for marrying."

"Even so——"

She looked me full in the face. "Even so what? What you planning on doing, girl?"

"I ain't—I'm not planning on anything 'cause I can't think of anything to plan on! I just don't want to look back. If they didn't like me before all this happened, they're sure not going to love me now. So what I was thinking was I might get a job. Go somewhere."

"So you thought you'd up and run away and find yourself a job, that what you thought, girl?" I recognized her I-ain't-gonna-listen-to-none-of-your-nonsense voice. "Well, now I'm right glad you told me 'cause ole Ruth can tell you something. I keeps a clean house, minds the chillun, and cooks the evening supper, and for doing all these things it takes me six workdays to earn seven dollars and fifty cents. Now how many of those things can you do? And how much you reckon you'd be earning for doing them?"

"There are other jobs."

"There's plenty more jobs. They got judges, doctors, and sheriffs. Which one you qualified for, girl?"

"There has to be something."

"There is something. Now, you listen hard 'cause Ruth gonna tell you jest like I'd tell my own child, which you is! You is goin' back home and finishing up with your high school education. Nevah you mind what folks say, most folks don't know what they is saying nohow. Then you tells your daddy that you wants to go way to college to be somethin'. And you bees somethin'! A teacher or a nurse, don't matter what you takes a notion to being as long as it's something."

"I know the something I'd like to be," I said, pausing just long enough to build interest. "A reporter. I already have my first assignment and my *nom de plume* too."

"Your what?"

"*Nom de plume.* Pen name. What do you think of Antonia Alexander?"

"Antonia Alexander," repeated Ruth, like she was tasting the words. "Mighty fancy."

I was pleased that its elegance hadn't escaped her.

"I got the Antonia from Anton, and I picked Alexander because of the alliteration, both names starting with the same letter."

"What is you fixin' to write?"

"An article about the conditions at the Bolton Reformatory for the *Memphis Commercial Appeal*." I checked Ruth's face to see if she was as impressed as I was. "Charlene Madlee said if it was good, they'd run the story in their Arkansas edition."

"I'se glad, Honey Babe. You shore is gonna be somethin'." Ruth gave a sigh filled with pride for my future accomplishments. "And then you won't have to go home ever again, less'n you want to."

"I guess sometime I'll have to come home again to see you."

I heard the footsteps first and then the rattling of keys.

Mis Laud appeared in the archway. "Visiting time is over. Separate and leave immediately."

"Not yet, Miss Laud, please. Ruth just now got here."

"She has been here for thirty minutes. Her time is up. Leave immediately."

I knew I was going to beg. "Miss Laud, please, she came so far. She's the only visitor I've had since I've been here, and she's the only one I'm gonna get, I know." The cracks sounded in my voice.

"Miss Laud, if you'd kindly be so kind—" Ruth knew what to say. She'd listen to Ruth—"as to give us a few more minutes to say our last minute things, that'd help make the parting less hurtful."

Miss Laud's eyes jumped, all the time jumping from Ruth to me and back again. Something about them I saw for the first time. There was the palest circle of blue surrounding pupils the size of points on an ice pick. Miss Laud raised a trembling finger and pointed it toward me. "That's why you're in trouble. Not happy getting what others got, are you?" She shook her head.

"Trouble is you're a greedy, spoiled girl. Don't like anything we try to give you, do you? Don't like our religion, don't like our laundry, and you don't think our food is worth eating. You told that to one of the girls, didn't you? Tell the truth!"

She waited for me to answer her charges, but the only answer I gave was a direct stare.

She wet her lips with her tongue. "Truth is you only like Nigras and Nazis!"

"Miss Laud!" said Ruth in as loud a voice as I'd ever heard her use. "Leave the child alone! I'se goin' now. See me goin'?"

I threw my arms around Ruth's neck. "Take me with you. Find a way to take me with you!"

"Shush, Honey Babe, shush now."

"Don't leave me here, Ruth! Please, please don't leave me alone."

"Honey Babe, you know better'n to ask Ruth to do what she jest ain't got the power to do." Ruth patted my cheeks as she wiped away the wetness. "Everything gonna be all right," she whispered. "One fine day, you is gonna wake up and your heart gonna rise up singing, everything gonna be all right."

"Wallace!" shouted Miss Laud. "Wallace, Rogers! Here! Come here!"

I hung onto Ruth with all my might; she was my life raft and without her the icy waters were waiting to pull me under.

Footsteps raced across linoleum. As Matron Wallace and Matron Rogers came through the archway Ruth raised her hand as though she were stopping traffic. "You leave this child be! Now, I'm a-telling you, jest *leave* this child be!"

The traffic stopped short. The matrons looked as though their very breath had been sucked out of them.

"Jest seems like," said Ruth under her breath, yet loud enough for hearing, "some white folks ain't nevah learned how to be decent."

196

And with her arm around my waist and her strength supporting my weakness she led me through the archway and into the center hall. "Go on back to your room, Patty Babe," she whispered. "Go on back."

The three matrons had followed us at a respectful distance, but Miss Laud's distance was the most respectful of all. Suddenly, Ruth whirled on her. "Miss Laud, the red shopping bag in the waiting room. Patty's Christmas. Would you fetch it, please?"

The head matron looked confused. She turned to Matron Wallace. "Well, get it, Wallace! Don't just stand there. Go get the bag!" Then Miss Laud started up the flight of stairs followed closely by Miss Rogers.

As soon as Miss Wallace dropped the bag at Ruth's feet she took the stairs, two at a time. And it was just Ruth and me.

"I reckon they is gonna give us our good-bye time, after all," said Ruth.

I tried to sound all put back together. "Well, Ruth, I sure do appreciate your visit."

She gave me some gentle pats on the back. "And you be strong and don't let them folks get you down 'cause better times a-coming for you. I feels it in my bones."

"Do you really? You really and truly think so?"

"I shore enough do."

Yet Ruth's face was filled with the deepest kind of sadness.

"And for you, Ruth, are better times coming for you too?"

"Mostly things don't get no better for old colored ladies."

"Oh, but I want them to be. I want everything to be good for you. Everything!"

She turned her head. "Good-bye, Honey Babe." She released her hold on me and where her arms had been turned cold. It felt as though something inside me were being torn away. I watched her walk with careful steps back to the bench where she had left her belongings. And watching her, she seemed older and more fragile than I had remembered.

Suddenly I had to give her something, something like the world! I quickly indexed the valuables from my upstairs room—the blue Schaeffer pen and pencil set (a birthday present from my grandparents), a collection of the short stories of Guy de Maupassant, and *Webster's Collegiate Dictionary*. Nothing there for Ruth. She moved slowly towards the door, buttoning her gray coat.

"I don't have anything to give you," I said. "I have nothing at all to give you."

"You got love to give, Honey Babe, ain't nothing better'n that."

"Just the same, I wish I could—say, how about taking back some of the chicken breasts to eat on the bus?"

She clicked open her simulated alligator pocketbook, giving me a view of the inside. "I got me a tunafish sandwich and a hard-boiled egg, and I reckon that's plenty for me. Thank you kindly." Then Ruth reached out, patted my cheek, and with aging steps moved towards the door.

I watched her. It was like watching my very own life raft floating away towards the open sea. And yet somewhere in my mind's eye I thought I could see the faintest outline of land. Then it came to me that maybe that's the only thing life rafts are supposed to do. Taking the shipwrecked, not exactly to the land, but only in view of land. The final mile being theirs alone to swim.

As Ruth pulled open the heavy front door my heart felt as though it was spilling over with so many things I wanted to say, but I didn't have the words for a single one of them. For a moment I thought I was about to call out, "Good-bye," but I didn't. The door closed. And the moment and Ruth were gone.

For moments or minutes I stood there. Not really moving. Barely managing to tread water. Was it possible for a beginning swimmer to actually make it to shore? It might take me my whole lifetime to find out.

ABOUT THE AUTHOR

BETTE GREENE grew up in a small Arkansas town and in Memphis, Tennessee. She studied in Paris and in New York, where she was a student of Martha Foley's at Columbia University. She has published short stories and newspaper and magazine articles. Her other novels include the sequel *Morning Is a Long Time Coming; Philip Hall Likes Me, 1 Reckon Maybe* and *Get on Out of Here, Philip Hall.* Mrs. Greene now lives in Brookline, Massachusetts, with her husband and two children.

STARFIRE

POWERFUL STORIES
OF SELF-DISCOVERY

☐ **NOTHING IN COMMON**
   by Barbara Bottner   **27060-5 $2.95**

Melissa and Sara live in such different worlds that it's hard for either one to believe that they will ever have anything in common. But when unexpected tragedy occurs, their worlds collide with astounding results!

☐ **SUMMER OF MY GERMAN SOLDIER**
   by Bette Greene   **27247-0 $2.95**

Awkward, lonely Patty Bergen was twelve the summer that the World War II German prisoners arrived at the POW camp outside Jenkinsville, Arkansas. Then she meets Anton, a German prisoner. A strong and dangerous friendship develops and changes their lives *forever*.

☐ **MORNING IS A LONG TIME COMING**
   by Bette Greene   **27354-X $2.95**

In this sequel to SUMMER OF MY GERMAN SOLDIER, Patty Bergen is eighteen. The townspeople have not forgiven her for her loyalty to Anton, the German soldier. When she graduates from high school Patty decides to go to Germany to meet Anton's family. But it is in Paris that she finds the love that helps her make peace with her past.

Special Offer
Buy a Bantam Book
for only 50¢.

Now you can order the exciting books you've been wanting to read straight from Bantam's latest catalog of hundreds of titles. *And* this special offer gives you the opportunity to purchase a Bantam book for only 50¢. Here's how:

By ordering any five books at the regular price per order, you can also choose any other single book listed (up to a $5.95 value) for only 50¢. Some restrictions do apply, so for further details send for Bantam's catalog of titles today.

Just send us your name and address and we'll send you Bantam Book's SHOP AT HOME CATALOG!